Callie's Christmas Wish

Merline Lovelace

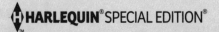

Recycling programs
for this product may
not exist in your area.

ISBN-13: 978-0-373-65994-4

Callie's Christmas Wish

Copyright © 2016 by Merline Lovelace

Printed in U.S.A.

www.Harlequin.com

He knew exactly where to find her

Watching the Trevi Fountain come to life, water spilling from it into the basin.

"Callie."

Her hips swiveled. Her head turned. Those soul-stripping eyes locked with his. "Hello, Joe. Tracking me down again?"

"We need to talk."

She gave a short laugh. "I thought that was my line."

He sat beside her on the edge of the fountain.

"Do you remember the last time we were here?" she asked after a moment, her gaze on the glistening water.

"I remember."

"I made a wish then. Should I tell you what it was?"

Joe wasn't sure he wanted to know. When he made a noncommittal sound, she angled her chin and pinned him with those incredible eyes.

"I wished for a dreamy romantic hero right out of the movies," she confessed.

"Sorry. Looks like you're zero for three." He didn't see himself as dreamy or romantic or heroic.

"Maybe I should make another wish." Eyes closed, she looked as though she was sorting through dozens of possibilities before settling on one. Then she sent the coin sailing toward the fountain.

"What did you wish for this time?"

She smiled. "You'll just have to wait and see."

THREE COINS IN THE FOUNTAIN:
When you wish upon your heart...

Dec 16

Dear Readers,

Okay, now be honest! Can you think of anything more exciting and romantic and colorful than Christmas in Rome? Except Christmas at home with your family and friends, of course. I've loved writing each book in the Three Coins In the Fountain series, but this one was such fun because it let me vicariously indulge in so many wonderful Italian holiday traditions. The food, the lights, the gorgeously hand-crafted crèches—I was right there with Callie and Joe that whole time.

Incidentally, Callie's side trip to the buffalo ranch was based on actual research I did during a cruise stop in Naples. I found the whole mozzarella-production process so fascinating that I took extensive notes and knew I *had* to work it into a book someday. Luckily, Joe just happened to have business that took him to Naples!

I hope you enjoy reading *Callie's Christmas Wish* as much as I did writing it...and may all *your* Christmas wishes come true, too!

Merline Lovelace

A career Air Force officer, **Merline Lovelace** served at bases all over the world. When she hung up her uniform for the last time, she decided to try her hand at storytelling. Since then, more than twelve million copies of her books have been published in over thirty countries. Check her website at merlinelovelace.com or friend Merline on Facebook for news and information about her latest releases.

Many, many thanks to Machaelie Halsey,
who let me pick her brain about
counseling techniques during lunch at Chili's,
then read several chapters while we were
cooking Easter dinner. Thanks, too,
to Christy Gronlund, who filled me in on the joys and
stresses of Children's Advocacy. You both made this
book so rich in detail and rewarding for me to write.

Chapter One

It started with the fountain.

That damned Trevi Fountain.

Callie and her two best friends *had* to take a long-dreamed-of trip to Italy this past September. Then she and Dawn and Kate *had* to defy the tradition that said just tossing a coin in the fountain would bring them back to Rome someday. Oh, no. The centuries-old tradition wasn't good enough. They *had* to make separate, secret wishes.

Kate's came true while the three friends were still in Italy, when she and her husband reconciled mere weeks away from a divorce. Dawn didn't realize her wish had been granted until she was back in the States and acting as surrogate nanny for a lively six-year-old. A few short weeks later, the laughing, flirtatious redhead had made the surprising and completely unexpected leap from carefree bachelorette to deliriously happy mother to Tommy and wife to hunky Brian Ellis.

Callie had made a wish in Rome, as well. One she hadn't shared with anyone. Not even her BFFs. It was too silly, too frivolous. And so not in keeping with her usual level-headed self.

That ridiculous wish was coming back to haunt her now. Every part of her thrummed with nervous anticipation as she helped Dawn and Tommy loop fresh pine boughs into Christmas wreaths for the doors of the Ellises' home. Luckily, the determined efforts of Tommy's three-month-old wheaten terrier pup to get into the action kept both the boy and Dawn so amused that neither noticed Callie jump when the doorbell rang.

The sound of the bell sent the pup into an immediate frenzy. His butt end whipped around. His claws skittered on the pine plank flooring. High-pitched yelps split the air as he careened out of the kitchen and down a hallway fragrant with the scent of the cloves and cinnamon and oranges in the Christmas potpourri.

"That'll be Joe."

Pushing to her feet, Dawn dusted the pine needles from the moss-colored turtleneck that clung to her generous curves and made her eyes appear an even deeper shade of emerald.

"His message said his plane would touch down at three and he'd be here by four." She slanted Callie a sly look. "Tall, dark, handsome *and* punctual. What more could a girl ask for?"

Nothing, Callie agreed, her stomach fluttering. Not a single, solitary thing.

Except…maybe…

There it was! That absurd coin toss again. How juvenile to wish Joe would let just a tiny smidgen of romance sneak through his solid, masculine, don't-mess-with-me-or-mine exterior. Hadn't he put his highly lucrative business interests on hold for her? Devoted considerable time and expense to tracking down the source of the ugly emails she'd begun receiving a few weeks before the trip to Italy? Shaking her head at her own foolishness, Callie followed Dawn, the wildly yipping terrier and Tommy down the hall.

"Joe promised he'd bring me a real, live boomerang from Australia," the boy reminded them as he charged for the door. "Hope he remembered it!"

He would. Callie didn't doubt it for a second. In the few short months she'd known Joe Russo, she'd come to realize that nothing ever escaped the steel trap of his mind.

They'd first met during a never-to-be-forgotten jaunt to Venice. At the time Joe headed a highly specialized personal security team guarding Carlo Luigi Francesco di Lorenzo, aka the Prince of Lombard and Marino, who also happened to be one of Italy's most decorated air force pilots. Carlo, Kate's husband, Travis, and Dawn's now-husband, Brian, had been involved in testing some hush-hush, super-secret modification to NATO special ops aircraft flying sorties from a base in northern Italy.

Callie and Joe had met again in Rome, when Travis surprised Kate with an elegant ceremony to renew their marriage vows. At that damned fountain! It must have been the stars in Kate's eyes as she reaffirmed her love. Or the mischievous sparkle in Dawn's when she announced she was flying home with the Ellises to assume duties as Tommy's stand-in nanny. Whatever the impetus, Callie gave in to her friends' urging that they all toss one last coin over their shoulders. Which was when she'd made that stupid, *stupid* wish.

Not ten minutes later, she'd found herself separated

from her friends and yielding to Joe Russo's quiet but relentless interrogation. As she'd soon discovered, the man hadn't transitioned from military cop to soldier of fortune to head of one of the world's most exclusive personal protection agencies without learning how to extract secrets from even the most reluctant interviewees.

He'd watched her, Joe had revealed. Saw how her shoulders braced every time she checked her email. Noted, too, how her eyes would flicker with distress before she withdrew even farther into her seemingly serene shell.

Callie tried to deny it. Tried to shrug aside his laser-sharp perceptions. She was too used to safeguarding the privacy of the children she'd represented as an ombudsman for the Massachusetts Office of the Child Advocate to spill their—or her—secrets. At that point Joe reminded her that she'd walked away from her job some weeks ago. He also pointed out that he could tap into any legal and/ or law enforcement agencies necessary to resolve whatever was scaring the crap out of her.

Callie still couldn't believe she'd broken down and told him about the threatening emails before she'd shown them to Kate and Dawn. Neither could her two best friends, for that matter. They'd let her know what they thought about that in some pretty forceful terms. But they got over their snit in short order and promptly threw a protective shield around her.

First, Kate insisted Callie stay with her in DC after their return from Italy. Then, when Dawn married and moved out of the elegant gatehouse designed for Tommy's live-in nanny, *she'd* insisted Callie take up residence there while Joe investigated the emails. And when the emails escalated from ugly to really scary, Joe tried to hustle her into protective custody.

Callie had drawn the line at that. She was staying in DC, hundreds of miles from her Boston home. She had four fierce watchdogs in the persons of Kate and Dawn and their spouses guarding her day and night. She'd turned over every threatening communication to the authorities, and Joe had exercised the legal system to gain access to the juvenile court cases she'd worked.

Enough was enough.

But her heart had still pounded each time she checked her emails. It pounded even harder every time Joe called or flew in to update her on his investigation. The kiss he'd laid on her last time he was in DC might also have something to do with the fact that she was holding her breath while Tommy yanked open the front door.

"Hi, Joe. Didja bring the boomerang? Didja?"

"You bet."

One of Joe's rare smiles flickered across his face. His cheeks creased, almost hiding the scar slashing down the left side. All Callie knew was that it was the legacy of a mission he wouldn't talk about to anyone, not even to Brian, Travis or Carlo. The angry red slash had faded in the past few months but still drew occasional startled glances.

Callie barely noticed it anymore. The rest of the package was too compelling. The broad shoulders now encased in a leather bomber jacket that had seen its share of wear, the square chin, the ice-gray eyes, the dark brown hair with its barest hint of a curl.

"Don't forget what I told you," Joe instructed as he stepped through the door and handed over a package wrapped in brown paper. "It's not a toy."

"I remember! Boomerangs are more than ten thousand years old. The aber...um...abra..."

"Aborigines."

"Yeah. The aborigines used to hunt with 'em."

While the boy tore at the brown paper, Joe nodded hello to Dawn before shifting his gaze to Callie. In their short time together, she'd discovered that his silvery eyes could turn as opaque and impenetrable as a Massachusetts coastal fog when he wanted, which was most of the time. But they glinted now with a triumph so clear and sharp that she knew instantly his sudden trip Down Under had yielded results.

"The emails!" she exclaimed. "You nailed the sender."

"To the wall," he replied with such savage satisfaction that Dawn whooped and flung up a palm for a joyous high five.

"All riiiight, Russo!"

The exuberant exclamation startled Tommy and the pup. Blue eyes wide, the boy clutched his boomerang to his chest and demanded to know what was going on while his pet made indiscriminate lunges at any and all adults.

"Down!"

Joe's low command caught the terrier in midlunge. It dropped instantly onto its haunches, looking as uncertain as a cuddly, curly-haired puppy could.

"Let me take your jacket," Dawn said in the sudden, blessed silence. "Then we'll go into the kitchen and you can tell us every detail."

"Mooooom."

Tommy stretched the single syllable into a mile-long protest that stopped Dawn in her tracks. Despite the butterflies in her stomach, Callie had to smile at her friend's goofy expression. The bubbly, irrepressible Dawn still wasn't used to being a mother to anyone, much less a blue-eyed imp with the face of an angel and enough energy to propel the Hubble Space Telescope into extended orbit.

"Joe's gotta show me how to make my boomerang come back," Tommy insisted. "Or…" He assumed an air of patently false innocence. "I guess I could take it outside and figure out how it works myself."

"Yeah," Dawn snorted. "Like I'm going to turn you loose with an ancient hunting weapon."

The Ellises' home was in an older part of Bethesda, just over the Maryland border from Washington, DC. The neighborhood consisted of gracious brick and stone houses set on large, tree-shaded lots. Their backyard was enclosed in mellow brick and graced by a fanciful gazebo now dusted with a light snow. It was also overlooked by a half dozen plate-glass windows, all of which were at risk despite Tommy's assurances that he would be *real* careful.

"We want to hear Joe's news," Dawn told the boy firmly. "Then we'll all put on our jackets and go out with you."

His lower lip jutted mutinously. "But…"

"Chill, dude."

Always a man of few words, Joe got his point across without raising his voice. Dawn flashed him a rueful smile as she created a diversion for boy and dog.

"Why don't you go into the den and get on the computer? You can pull up that website on the aerodynamics of boomerang flight your dad bookmarked for you. I bet Joe would like to see it after we talk."

Reluctant but outnumbered, Tommy caved. "'Kay. Just don't talk too long."

Still clutching his prize, he scampered off with the pup hard on his heels. Joe shrugged out of his jacket and raised a brow as Dawn hooked the well-worn leather on the hall coatrack.

"Aerodynamics of flight, huh?"

"What can I say? Brian and his first wife were both engineers. It's in Tommy's genes."

It was a measure of Dawn's basic warmth and security in her two-month-old marriage that she didn't want Tommy to forget his birth mother. Caroline Ellis had died of a brain tumor less than a year after her son's birth. Tommy had no real memories of her except those captured in the exquisite digital book Dawn had made for him using all her skills as a graphic designer.

"C'mon. I'll brew you some coffee while you tell us all."

Dawn turned to lead the way down the hall, so she missed the casual hand Joe laid at the small of her friend's back. Callie, on the other hand, felt the light touch right through her baggy purple sweater and cotton camisole.

When Joe called to say his plane had touched down, she'd almost dashed to the gatehouse to change, slap on some lip gloss and drag a brush through her mink-brown hair. She'd been thinking about taking Dawn's advice and getting the shoulder-length mass shaped at one of DC's elegant salons. With her life pretty much on hold these past weeks, though, she'd settled for just pulling it back in a ponytail or clipping it up.

She made a futile effort to tuck back some of the wayward strands as she and Joe settled in high-backed stools at the kitchen counter and Dawn plugged a fresh, single-cup, dark arabica blend container into the coffeemaker. As hot water steamed through the cup, the coffee's rich aroma competed with the sappy tang of the fresh-cut pine boughs on the kitchen table.

"Okay," Dawn demanded when the super-fast appliance delivered a steaming mug. "Talk! We've all been speculating like crazy since you took off so suddenly for Sydney. Tell us who the creep is who's been sending those emails and why."

Joe swiveled to face Callie. "Do you remember acting as ombudsman for a girl named Rose Graham?"

Frowning, she flipped through a mental filing cabinet of the cases she'd worked in her six years with the Massachusetts Office of the Child Advocate. Some files were slender; others were fat and crammed with tragic details. Still others were truly horrific. As best Callie could recall, though, Rose Graham's case file was one of the thinner ones.

"I remember the name."

"She was five when her parents duked it out in divorce court."

From the corner of her eye Callie saw an all-too-familiar mask slip over Dawn's normally expressive face. Her friend had been a young teen when her parents' increasingly bitter arguments led to an even more acrimonious divorce, with their only daughter caught smack in the middle. Kate and Callie had acted as buffers as much as possible, but sharing Dawn's heartache had been a significant factor in Callie's decision to pursue a master's degree in family psychology and accept an appointment as a children's advocate.

"The mother worked as a paralegal," Joe prompted. "The father was a software developer at one of Boston's ultra-high-tech medical research companies."

The details seeped back. Callie could visualize Rose Graham—fair-haired, small for her age and very bright.

"I remember the case now." Her forehead crinkled. "As best I recall, it was pretty open-and-shut. The child was well adjusted, doing fine in preschool and clearly adored by both parents. Judges are predisposed to leave a female child that young with the mother unless there's evidence of gross neglect or abuse. But…" Her frown deepened. "I'm pretty sure I recommended generous visitation rights for the father."

"You did, which was why we didn't give the Graham case as much scrutiny as some of the others. Only after I had my people go back and do a second scrub did we learn the father's company transferred him to their Australian office earlier this year."

"Uh-oh."

With a sinking sensation, Callie sensed what was coming. Otherwise amicable divorce and custody agreements could turn ugly when overseas travel was involved. The cost of the travel itself was often prohibitive, and the court couldn't discount the possibility a child taken outside its jurisdiction would not be returned. For that reason, Callie's report to the judge had contained the standard caveat requiring review if either of the parents should relocate outside the US.

"Rose's mother flat refused to let her daughter fly all the way to Australia," Joe confirmed.

"And the law firm she worked for tied her ex up in legal knots," Callie guessed. She'd seen that too many times, too.

"The father had to come back to the States so often for hearings and court appearances that he wiped out his savings and was forced to take out huge loans. As a result, he fell behind on child support."

Callie grimaced. "And that in turn led the state to institute proceedings to garnish his wages from his home company in Boston, only adding to his legal woes and burden of debt."

"He asked his company to transfer him back to Boston. He's been waiting for six months for a position to open up."

"In the meantime, his anger at the system festered."

"And then some." Joe shook his head in disgust. "I can't believe it took my people so long to break through the series of firewalls he erected. The man's damned good at what he does."

"But your people are better," Dawn commented.

"That's why I pay 'em the big bucks."

"So what happened when you confronted Graham?" she wanted to know.

"Pretty much what I'd expected. He acted astonished, then indignant. Then, when the Aussie cybercrimes detectives who accompanied me to his place of employment laid out the electronic evidence, he wouldn't say another word without an attorney present. After his lawyer showed up it still took some persuasion," Joe said with what both women suspected was considerable understatement, "but he finally admitted to fixating on the caveat in Callie's report as the root cause of his problems."

"Right," Dawn snorted. "Not the judge who signed the visitation order. Not his ex-wife or her team of lawyers. And of course not himself."

"Of course." Joe's silver-gray eyes frosted with icy satisfaction. "Bastard's in a world of hurt now. He'll be sitting in a cell for months while the US and Australia work out jurisdictional issues. Years, maybe, since the investigation and prosecution of terror-related cybercrimes takes far higher precedence in both countries than his threats."

Callie might have felt sorry for Rose's father if his vicious emails hadn't disrupted her life for the past three months. She'd have to pick up the pieces and get on with it, she realized. But first…

"Thank you." Reaching across the counter, she laid a hand over Joe's. "I appreciate all you've done for me. More than I can ever say. I hated involving you in the mess, but…"

"Hated me butting in, you mean."

"Well, yes. At first." She had to smile. "After all, we barely knew each other."

"A situation I've been trying to remedy."

He had. He most definitely had. Just remembering the hard press of his mouth on hers the evening before his sudden trip to Australia brought a wash of heat from the neck of her sweater. The heat surged even higher when Joe turned his hand, enfolded hers and brushed his thumb over her wrist in slow, easy strokes.

Callie didn't dare glance at her friend. Dawn wasn't the least bit hesitant to dish out advice or offer opinions. She and Kate had both already suggested—several times!—that strong, silent, super-macho Joe Russo had a serious case of the hots for the quiet, seemingly demure member of their trio.

Thankfully Dawn refrained from commenting on either Joe's thumb movements or the heat now spreading across Callie's cheeks. Instead she invented a quick excuse to depart the scene.

"I'd better go make sure Tommy isn't trying to test those aerodynamic principles in the den. Give a shout when you're ready to, uh, take the action outside."

The door to the den swished shut behind her, and a sudden silence descended. Callie was the first to break it. Her hand still in Joe's, she tried to ignore the skitter of nerves his stroke was generating and smiled up at him.

"I meant what I just said, Joe. I'm really, really grateful. And so relieved it's finally over."

"Me, too. It's been keeping me awake at night."

"I've lost sleep, too," she admitted. "I can't ever repay you for the man-hours you and your people put into the investigation."

"If it gets the shadows out of your eyes, I'll consider the debt paid."

His gaze locked on hers. "Your eyes are the damnedest color," he said after a small pause. "Not purple, not lavender. Sort of halfway between the two. First thing I noticed about you."

Well, Callie thought with an inner grimace, it wouldn't have been her ebullient personality or luscious curves. Dawn had the corner on those. And any stray male glances the flamboyant redhead didn't instantly capture, Kate's lustrous, sun-streaked blond hair and mile-long legs would.

"Thanks," she said for lack of a better response.

"I tried to find the right way to describe the color when I gave my folks your vitals," he said with a rueful grimace. "Couldn't bring myself to go with hyacinth or heliotrope. Their jaws would've smacked their chests."

Callie's own jaw almost took a trip south. These were the most words she'd heard Joe string together in one sitting. They were also the most surprising.

"So what *did* you go with?"

"Pansy."

Her nose wrinkled. "Lovely."

"Yeah, they are."

His hand tightened and tugged her closer. His other hand came up to slide under her hair. His palm felt warm on her nape, the skin hard and ridged in spots. She'd once read that expert marksmen fired thousands of rounds weekly to maintain their skills and developed shooter's calluses as a result.

Okay. She'd read that just a few weeks ago. When she was trying to weave a more complete picture of Joe Russo from the scant threads of his past that he'd shared with her. She was thinking of the still-gaping holes in that picture when he reclaimed her attention with a gruff admission.

"Those damned emails weren't the only thing keeping me awake."

He lowered his head but didn't swoop in and catch her by surprise, as he had the night before his abrupt departure for Australia. He gave her plenty of time to pull away, to ease out of his loose grip. So much time she was the one who leaned into the kiss.

That was all the encouragement he needed. With a low grunt, he pushed off his stool. She came off hers eagerly. The hand still wrapped around her nape moved up. He tipped her head back for a better angle and used his other arm to fit her against him. She strained even closer while his mouth worked hard, hungry magic on hers.

Within moments, Callie was aching for more. She wanted him out of his shirt. Out of his worsted-wool slacks and his Italian leather boots and…

"Caaal-lee."

She jerked her back and looked over her shoulder to find Tommy glaring at them with equal parts indignation and accusation. His pup wedged through the door with him and yipped, as if wanting to add his two cents to whatever was going on.

"Mom said you guys were still talking. But you're not. You're kissing 'n' stuff."

They hadn't actually gotten to the "stuff" part, but

Callie was thinking about it. Thinking hard. So was Joe, judging by the wicked tilt to his mouth.

"Yeah," he admitted, "we are."

Scowling, Tommy planted his fists on his hips. "When are you gonna be done?"

Joe slanted Callie a wry look. "How about we finish our...discussion...later? Somewhere private. Inaccessible to kids and dogs."

"Deal."

"All right, kid. Get your jacket and your boomerang and we'll go outside."

Chapter Two

When Joe stepped outside, he welcomed the clean, sharp bite of a DC winter. December was midsummer in Australia. During his flying visit, Sydney had been sweltering through usually high temperatures. As a result he enjoyed the brisk chill almost as much as he did Tommy the Terrible's determination to get his boomerang to fly.

Before making the first attempt, though, the boy fingered the fine-grained wood surface and gravely explained its aerodynamic principles to Joe. "See, this is a nonballistic missile."

"That so?"

"Uh-huh. It's different from ballistic missiles. They're, like, spears 'n' arrows 'n' bullets 'n' stuff. When you throw them or shoot them from a gun, they fly up in an arc till gravity pulls them down."

Which was about as cogent a distillation of ballistics as Joe had ever heard. He hid a grin as he thought of the hours he'd spent on the range as a raw recruit learning to calculate distance, velocity and trajectory.

"But a boomerang's different," Tommy continued, his face a study in fierce concentration as he fingered the intricate designs inlaid in the wood. "It's got this curved shape 'n' wide surface 'n' the top is conver... convey..."

"Convex?"

"Yeah, convex. Anyway, Dad says if you throw it right, it'll defy gravity as long as it has enough speed 'n' the rotation will bring it right back to you."

"Sounds like you've got the theory down. Want to put in practice?"

"Yes!"

Thankfully, Joe's Aussie contact had directed him to an indigenous arts and crafts store with a very accommodating owner. The man had hooked a Closed sign in his shop window and taken his customer to the soccer field just a half block from his store. It took patient coaching and several attempts before Joe eventually got the damned boomerang to return.

The Ellises' backyard wasn't anywhere near as large as a soccer field, but Joe figured it was adequate for Tommy's strength and throwing ability. Hunkering down on his heels, he shared his recently acquired knowledge.

"Okay, hold it in a two-fingered pistol grip."

"Huh?"

"Sorry. Hold it here with your thumb and two fingers. Tuck the other fingers into your fist. Good. Now lift the boomerang vertical to your shoulder. A little higher. Okay. It doesn't take a lot of effort to throw this. Just bring your arm back and hurl it forward."

Tommy's first attempt sent the boomerang plowing

straight down into the snow-dusted grass. The second whizzed past the pup's nose. The third actually flew off to the right, whirled and started to return before it ran out of speed.

"Joe! It was coming back!"

"I saw."

Thrilled with his throw, Tommy almost tripped over his pet in his eagerness to retrieve the boomerang. Joe figured he'd pretty well exhausted his expertise and leaned against the garden wall to let the boy enjoy himself.

He was a good kid. Make that a great kid.

Looking back, Joe could admit he'd harbored more than a few doubts when he'd heard Brian Ellis had brought his young son to Italy. At the time, Ellis, USAF Major Travis Westbrook and the playboy prince Joe and his team were providing special security for were in the final test phase of a highly classified NATO special ops aircraft modification. The mod had been designed by Ellis Aeronautical Systems, however, and the company's CEO was a widower who included his son and the boy's nanny on extended trips abroad whenever he could. Unfortunately, the nanny tripped and broke her ankle in the final and most critical phase of the test.

Joe didn't believe in luck. Not many men and women in his profession did. You considered every possible contingency, devised backup plans, worked out alternate escape routes and relied on training and instinct to get you out of tight situations. He was living proof that the formula worked...most of the time. When he looked in the mirror, however, he saw a graphic reminder of Curaçao and the one time his instincts were dead wrong.

Yet even he had to admit that chance or luck or whatever the hell you wanted to call it had played out in Italy. Kate and Travis Westbrook had hooked up again.

Fiery-haired Dawn McGill had stepped in as Tommy's temporary nanny. And Joe had met Callie Langston.

It hadn't been love at first sight. Not even, Joe recalled, instant lust. Callie would be the first to admit that most male glances slid right past her to snag on long-legged, tawny-haired Kate or laughing, flirtatious, extremely stacked Dawn.

Joe had experienced the same initial testosterone spike when introduced to the other two women. Right up until Callie had turned her head and nailed him with those purple eyes. But it wasn't until he saw her trying to disguise her reaction to those emails that she snagged more than a casual interest.

At first it was the cop in him. The military-trained investigator turned covert operator turned personal security expert. Then it was her insistence she could handle the problem herself. Then…

"Didja see that one, Joe? Didja?"

"I did. Good job, kid."

Then, Joe remembered, it was Brian and Dawn setting sparks off each other. And Kate and Travis getting back together. And the playboy prince putting the moves on Callie.

Carlo's heavy-handed seduction attempts had pissed Joe off more than they should have. They also got him thinking about things he hadn't allowed himself think about since Curaçao. Like someone to come home to. Hell, a *home* to come home to. And maybe, just maybe, a son like Tommy.

Suddenly impatient, Joe pushed away from the garden wall. "A couple more throws, kid."

"Not yet. I'm just gettin' good."

"Yes, yet. I want to finish talking to Callie. Besides," he added, taking a cue from Dawn's devious tactics, "your dad should be home soon. You don't want to wear out your arm before you show him your moves."

"'Kay. Four more."

"Two."

"Three."

"This one," Joe said in a tone that brooked no further argument, "and one more."

Inside the kitchen warmed by the dancing flames from a brick fireplace, Dawn and Callie cradled cups of steaming cappuccino and watched the action through frost-rimmed bay windows.

They'd just placed several calls. The first to Dawn's husband, Brian, to break the news that Joe had ID'd the originator of the emails. Another to the remaining member of their female triumvirate.

Kate had whooped with joy and relief and insisted they celebrate. Tonight. Before Joe disappeared again on one of his bodyguard gigs for some rock star or South American dictator. She and Travis would bring the champagne and sparkling cider. Dawn and Callie could take care of the eats.

They accomplished their assigned task by calling in a to-go order for tapas and paella at Paoli, a top-rated Mediterranean restaurant just a few blocks from the house. Which left them plenty of time to sip their cappuccinos and watch the outside activities.

"Joe's really good with Tommy," Dawn commented casually.

Too casually. Callie recognized that okay-whatever-I'm-just-saying tone. She buried her nose in the frothy brew and waited. Sure enough, Dawn plunked her own cup down and cut to the chase.

"C'mon, Cal. Give. To paraphrase my precocious little imp, what was with all that kissing 'n' stuff?"

Callie lowered her cup and met her friend's eager gaze. Her own, she knew, no doubt mirrored the welter of confusing emotions Joe Russo roused in her.

"I'm not sure. It's just... Well... Look, you've known Joe as long as I have."

"But not as well, obviously."

The drawled retort raised a smile, followed by a rueful grimace.

"The truth is, I don't know him as well as it might have appeared. Aside from the fact he can't—or won't—talk about his past, he's not exactly loquacious."

"No kidding. But back to that kiss. It wasn't the first, was it?"

"No."

"And?"

"And what?"

"Don't play innocent with me, sister. You might come across as all demure and innocent to outsiders, but Kate and I were peeking through the blinds when you sweet-talked Pimple Face Hendricks into dropping his drawers and showing off his prized possession."

"For pity's sake! We were, what? Eight or nine years old?"

"Old enough to know Pimple Face didn't have much to brag about. So spill it. Do you want Joe to deliver a repeat performance?"

There was only one answer to that. "Yes."

"Hallelujah! It's about time you took the plunge."

"Wait! I'm not exactly plunging into any—"

"The heck you're not. I can't count the number of studs Kate and I have fixed you up with in the past few years. After every date you've smiled your enigmatic

Mona Lisa smile and sent them on their way. Joe's the first male you've invited back for seconds."

"Dawn," Callie protested, half laughing and half embarrassed at how close that barb had hit to home. "It was only a kiss. Although…"

"Although what, Langston?"

She played with her half-empty cup. She couldn't understand her reluctance to share her silly wish with Dawn. God knows, they'd shared everything else in their lives. She hesitated another few seconds before yielding her secret.

"Okay, here's the deal. Remember when the three of us tossed coins in the Trevi Fountain that first time?"

"Of course I do. But you, Miss Priss and Boots, wouldn't make a wish. You insisted that just throwing in a coin satisfied tradition and we'd all return to Rome someday."

"Actually, I did make a wish."

"Which," Dawn guessed instantly, "involved Joe Russo."

"How could it? We didn't meet him until a week later, in Venice."

"Okay, okay. If you didn't wish for steamy, totally deviant sex with Mr. Macho out there, what was it? Please tell me it was something equally kinky."

"Since when are any of us into kink?"

When Dawn wagged her brows, Callie gave a rueful laugh. "All right. The wish was a little…fanciful."

"Are we talking satin sheets fanciful? Or whipped cream and melted chocolate? Or ice cubes and…"

"Dawn!"

"Ha! Do *not* go all prune-faced and prudish on me, missy. Just remember who advised Kate on the best brand of vibrator to buy when she and Travis separated."

"It was the same brand you recommend to me."

"Please stop annoying me with all these pesky details. Just tell me. What did you wish for?"

"Not what. Who. Louis Jourdan."

Dawn understood the reference instantly. She should, since she and Callie and Kate had drooled over the stunningly handsome '50s and '60s–era star during several all-night movie marathons as teens.

"God," Dawn breathed. "Do you remember him in *Gigi*? So suave and sophisticated and *hot*. The man made me want to jump straight from twelve to twenty."

"I think he was better in *Three Coins in the Fountain*," Callie mused.

She remembered the first time they'd watched the old classic. So many years ago. So many dreams ago.

"Did you ever notice how much Joe looks like him?"

That was met with a moment of startled silence.

"Now that you mention it," her friend said, recovering, "I can see the resemblance. Aside from that fact that Joe's eyes are gray, not brown, and he's probably four inches taller and considerably more muscled than our boy Louis, they're dead ringers."

"All right, I may be projecting a bit."

"Ya think? But, hey. Project away, girl. It's *so* romantic."

And *so* out of character. Despite the incident with Pimple Face Hendricks, Callie had always been the sensible, bookish one of the three. More into reading than boys in junior high. An honor student in high school. On scholarships all through college and her master's program.

Majoring in psychology had given her great insight into the vagaries of human behavior. Unfortunately, it had also reinforced her natural tendency to stand off to the side and observe. Six years at the child advocate's office, where she was sworn to protect her young clients' rights and privacy, had only added to her natural reticence. The often heartbreaking cases she'd worked had taught her to wall off her own emotions. Except, of course, from Kate and Dawn.

And now Joe.

He'd pierced her shell in Italy when he'd convinced her to tell him about the emails. He'd taken another whack at it with that kiss before he'd zipped down to Australia. The one he'd laid on her just a few moments ago had pretty well completed the conquest. Watching him now, coaching Tommy in the fine art of boomeranging, Callie could almost feel her outer barriers trembling like the fabled walls of Jericho.

"Well," Dawn commented in an obvious effort to validate Callie's wish at the fountain, "Joe certainly has what it takes to star in a few movies. They'd probably be more shoot-'em-up action flicks than romances, though." She hesitated a few moments. "It doesn't bother you, what he does?"

"It might, if I could pry more than the most superficial details about his clients out of him."

"Brian says Joe and his people were prepared to take a bullet for Carlo in Italy. Evidently the prince led a special ops raid that rescued some UN workers in Afghanistan. Or maybe it was Africa. Anyway, the group's leader put a bounty on Carlo's head. That's why he required beefed-up security when we first met him in Italy."

"Kate told me a little about that raid. Travis took part in it, too."

Dawn nodded. "I know I don't have to remind you that the constant fear and uncertainty, the never knowing where Travis was or how long he'd be gone or who was shooting at him, almost broke up Kate's marriage."

"No, you don't have to remind me."

Callie had been right there. She and Dawn both. Lending support and shoulders to cry on when Kate made the agonizing decision to end her marriage to the man she'd loved since high school. They'd been there, too, when Travis refused to let her go, insisting nothing else mattered if he didn't have her.

"Joe and I are nowhere near that stage," Callie said. "Or any stage, really."

"Tell that to your action hero." Dawn tilted her head in the direction of the window. "He looks like he has more than a kiss in mind."

Callie followed her nod and caught Joe's glance through the wide windows. He and Tommy and the pooch had finished and were heading in. When he jerked his chin in the direction of the gatehouse, she slid off the counter stool with more haste than grace.

"Kate said she'll leave work early," Callie reminded Dawn. "She and Travis should be here by six or six thirty."

"Brian's leaving early, too."

"Buzz me when they get here."

"You sure you want to be disturbed?"

Ignoring her friend's salacious grin, Callie met the three males at the back door. The pup danced around her while she dutifully praised Tommy's skills. Then Dawn lured her two boys into the main house with an offer of hot chocolate and whipped cream.

"Lots of whipped cream," she said with a wicked glance in Callie's direction.

Joe caught the less than subtle byplay. "Something going on I should know about?"

"Nothing important," she said as she led the way along the covered flagstone path to the gatehouse. Escaping the chill December air, she ushered him inside. "Here, let me take your coat."

She hung it beside hers on an empty hook. The well-worn bomber jacket carried his scent, she thought as she took a discreet sniff. Sharp and clean and leathery. It felt like him, too. Tough and resilient.

Oh, Lord! She had it worse than she thought if she was standing here smelling his jacket. Hoping to heck he hadn't witnessed the sniff test, she turned. Thankfully, he was looking around with interest.

"This is nice."

It was. Bright and cheerful, with floral chintzes and bay windows that invited the outside in. The gatehouse had provided Callie a cozy safe haven for almost two months now. She hated the idea of leaving but knew she had to pick up the threads of her life again.

The problem was, she had no desire to return to Boston or to her former career. Despite all the courses and training and advice to the contrary, she'd let too much of the heartache experienced by her young, helpless and too often abused clients get to her. Even before the emails, she'd decided to quit. Now all she had to do was figure out what to do with the rest of her life.

She had no idea how much Joe might play in that. If at all. The thought made her uncharacteristically nervous. To cover it, she responded to his comment with a lively patter.

"The Ellises had the whole gatehouse gutted and redone for Tommy's former nanny, Mrs. Wells. The one who broke her ankle in Venice. I don't think you met her."

"No, I didn't."

"Dawn's totally conflicted over that. She'd never wish anyone harm, but she wouldn't have met Brian and Tommy otherwise."

"And I wouldn't have met you."

Ohh-kay, Callie thought as he curled a knuckle under her chin. So much for small talk.

He tipped her face to his. "As I was saying before I got dragooned into boomerang duty, it wasn't just those damned emails keeping me awake these past weeks."

His voice got lower and huskier with each word. Combined with the brush of his thumb along her jaw, he managed to get every one of her nerves bucking.

"You're so beautiful."

The compliment touched a secret place deep inside her. She didn't lack confidence in herself or her abilities, but she'd spent a lifetime in Kate's and Dawn's more flamboyant shadows.

"When did you have your last eye exam?"

"I'm not talking the externals. I'm talking about what's inside. The quiet self-assurance. The serenity."

The happy glow faded a bit.

"I haven't felt all that self-assured or serene in the past few months."

"You hid it well, even from your best friends."

"There was so much happening in their lives. I didn't want to add to it."

"So you drew on your own inner strength, Callie. I admire that." His thumb made another pass. "You're the kind of woman I've been looking for. The kind I could come home to."

She didn't know why that doused the glow completely, but it did. She pulled back and searched his face. The scar didn't so much as enter into her thought process as she tried to interpret his expression.

It hit her a second later. Affection. That's what she was seeing. Admiration tinged with warm, genuine affection. Humiliatingly similar to what she saw on

Dawn's and Brian's faces when they played with their son's pup. The fact that Joe's was spiced with an unmistakable dollop of desire didn't soothe the swift, lancing hurt. Concealing her dismay, she eased out of his arms.

"Sorry, but I'm not sure I understand. What, exactly, do you mean by 'come home to'?"

"Well…" He paused, obviously searching for the right words and opted for a demonstration instead. "How about I just show you?"

He reached for her again and drew her closer. When his head lowered, Callie hesitated for just a moment before meeting him halfway. Her lips molded his. Her palms found his shoulders, circled his neck. It wasn't just affection, she told herself. She could taste his hunger, sense it in the arms that tightened around her waist.

When he widened his stance and positioned her between his thighs, she couldn't quite stifle a groan. She could feel him against her belly. A minor distraction at first. Then a hard, rampant bulge that shot heat from her midsection to every other part of her. She wanted this man. Ached for him. Would take him any way she could have him.

And when he scooped her into arms, she didn't hold back before responding to his gruff, "Which way to the bedroom?"

He undressed her with a skill that might have given Callie pause if she hadn't been so intent on matching him button for button, tug for tug. Her heart melted when he took time to sheathe himself. If she hadn't already been a little in love with him, his determination to protect her even in this most intimate act would've done the trick. That, and the fact that he drove her to sensual heights she'd never experienced before.

Every stroke, every kiss, every scrape of his late-afternoon bristles on her breasts and belly and thighs pushed her higher. She was panting when he parted her legs. Almost mindless with need when he entered her. Just enough sanity remained for her to take him along on the wild ride.

Her belly tight, she locked her calves around his. Her muscles contracted. *Every* muscle! She thrust her hips against his again, once more, and gave herself up to the roaring tide of sensation.

When they untangled, she came within a hair of succumbing to his offer of tomorrow and forever. Most likely would have, if he hadn't tucked her against him and stroked her hair. Slowly. Lazily. Again, with the same absent affection Dawn or Brian might stroke their son's puppy.

She didn't draw away. Didn't vocalize the return of her insidious doubts. Instead, she buried them deep as she and Joe took turns in the shower. He'd brought his carryall with him from the airport and changed into jeans and a misty-blue cashmere sweater that softened the steel gray of his eyes.

In deference to both the season and the occasion, Callie dressed up a bit in ballet flats, black tights with just a touch of silvery sparkle and a Christmassy green wool tunic. Twisting her hair up, she caught it with a jeweled butterfly clip she'd picked up on a foray to one of the DC area's many malls.

She was wearing her usual smile when she and Joe joined Dawn and Kate and their respective spouses to celebrate the end of her harassment.

Her calm smile stayed in place even when Kate and Dawn dragged her into the kitchen, using the excuse of making coffee for a tête-à-tête. Kate barely waited for the door to swish shut before she pounced.

"Details! The fat, pregnant sow wants details!"

Neither Dawn nor Callie bothered to point out that her tiny pooch barely even qualified as a baby bump.

"Rumor has it you and Joe got all close and cuddly this afternoon," Kate said. "Then you disappeared for several hours."

"Rumor being our gossipy friend here?"

"Hey!" Dawn protested. "Since when is any area of our lives off-limits? Seems like I can recall you two demanding every intimate detail when I got engaged the first time."

"And the second time," Kate admitted.

"And the third," Callie conceded.

"There! See? Turnabout's fair play. So how was it?"

"Pretty amazing, actually."

"You can do better than that, girl. On a scale of one to ten?"

"Twelve and a half."

"Way to go, Joe!"

Kate raised both palms and got slaps from the other women. Callie's was just a fraction slower than Dawn's, but the other two women picked up on that millisecond instantly.

"What?" Kate asked. "Twelve and a half didn't ring your bells?"

"They rang. Several times."

"But?"

She'd shared too many ups and downs with these women to hide her silly, niggling doubt from them. Still, she felt foolish even putting it into words.

"Turns out I want Louis Jourdan, and he wants Lassie."

Chapter Three

Dawn understood the reference to their earlier conversation, but Kate was totally confused. "Lassie? What's she got to...? Oh!" Her eyes popped. "Calissa Marie Langston, you sly thing! Just how kinky did you and Joe get this afternoon?"

"Kate! I was speaking metaphorically."

"Okay, now I'm really lost. How about translating for the verbally challenged? Where does Lassie come into this equation?"

Callie searched for the right words to frame her confused thoughts of a few hours ago. "Joe said I'm the kind of woman he could come home to. Not conquer worlds with. Not stand side by side with to battle the forces of evil."

"Okay," Kate said dubiously. "I guess that's a start."

"Some start," Dawn snorted. "I like Joe. What I know of him, anyway. And I love how good he is with Tommy. But he's not half as smart as I thought if he hasn't figured out Callie's the toughest one of the three of us."

"You and I know that," Kate agreed. "Travis, too. You gave him the most verbal abuse when he and I split, Dawn-O, but Callie sliced and diced him. The problem is, Joe hasn't seen that side of her."

"True." Dawn aimed a frown across the counter. "He stepped right into the role of big, strong hero to our helpless heroine. Okay, maybe not helpless," she amended when her friends opened their mouths on a simultaneous protest, "but you have to admit you haven't been yourself, Cal. Not since you quit your job." She cocked her head. "It wasn't just stress or the emails, was it?"

"No. I was... I don't know." She rubbed absently at a spot on the marble counter with a fingertip. "I guess the best way to describe it is feeling restless. As though life was passing me by. I needed a change."

"You don't think getting involved with Joe would provide enough of a change?"

"Yes. Of course it would." With a determined shrug, she shook off her odd mood. "Assuming, that is, he wants to get involved."

"Yeah, right," Kate drawled. "As if you *can* get more involved than twelve and a half."

"Maybe not," Callie agreed, laughing. "We'll see. In the meantime, we'd better put that coffee on and get back to the guys."

As much as Callie hated to admit it, Kate and Dawn were right. She *had* played the helpless heroine. Worse, she'd been more than willing to let Joe step right into the role of the big, strong protector while she hid out here in DC. It was time to take charge of her life again.

But first, she decided as her gaze rested on the man

she'd opened her arms and the quiet corners of her heart to, she needed to find out just where Joe thought things between them might go. That could well color her decision on where to live and what new career paths to explore.

She approached the issue in her characteristically straightforward way. Serene and unruffled on the outside and nervous as all hell inside, she invited Joe to the gatehouse after they'd finished their coffee. The door barely closed before he had her backed against it.

"I like your friends," he muttered, nuzzling her hair. "But they talk too much."

"It's…uh…called conversation."

Oh, for pity's sake! All the man had to do was blow in her ear and she stumbled over her own tongue.

"Not where I hail from," he countered as his lips grazed her cheek.

The gruff reply reminded Callie of her objective. "We need to talk about that, Joe."

He raised his head. "Where I hail from?"

"Among other things. Your security team dissected my life during the investigation. They checked out my Facebook friends. Where I buy my bagels. I don't know anything about you."

The withdrawal was so subtle, so slight. His expression didn't change. He still pressed hard against her. Yet Callie sensed a few degrees of separation instantly.

"What do you want to know?"

"More than I can absorb with my back up against a door and your mouth three inches from mine." She edged sideways. "Should I make another pot of coffee? Or would you like a brandy? Dawn left the bar pretty well stocked."

"I'm good."

"Okay. Well…"

She led the way into the combination living room, den and study. Like the rest of the gatehouse, it had been furnished with an eye for comfort and color. Periwinkle-blue hydrangeas and lilacs in full flower patterned the overstuffed sofa and easy chair. The sixty-inch TV was mounted at easy viewing level, and a small niche housed a built-in desk with hookups for all the latest electronic gadgets. As a tribute to both the season and the temporary nature of her occupancy, Callie had put up only a three-foot tree decorated with ornaments she and Tommy had made the previous Saturday morning.

Kicking off her ballet flats, Callie sank into the plush sofa cushions and tucked one foot under her. Joe took the opposite corner. She did her best to ignore the hard thighs and broad shoulders showcased to perfection by his jeans and that cloudy blue cashmere.

Joe met her gaze with a steady one of his own. "I can't tell you much, Callie. Most of the ops I participated in while I was in the military are still classified, and those I work for my clients are confidential."

"I'm more interested in the basics. Where's home?"

"Originally? A little town in Texas you never heard of."

"Try me."

"Bitter Creek."

"You're right. I've never heard of it. Did you leave there to go into the marines like Brian? Or was it the air force, like Travis?"

Again, his expression didn't change. Neither did his inflection. Yet Callie could sense the gap widening.

"Army. Rangers. Then," he added slowly, reluctantly, "Delta Force."

She had no idea who or what constituted Delta Force but decided she didn't really need to know at this point.

"How long were you in uniform?"

"Nine years."

Longer than she'd spent at the Office of the Child Advocate. Like her, Joe had changed direction in mid-career. More curious than ever, she probed deeper.

"Why did you leave the military?"

"It was time," he bit out.

Okay. That was obviously not something he wanted to talk about. Well, there was one subject he couldn't avoid. Raising a hand, she feathered a finger over his still fading scar.

"And this? Where did you get this?"

He froze her out. That's the only way she could describe it. The icy mask dropped over his face so swiftly, so completely, that she blinked.

"That's not open to discussion."

Joe smothered a curse when she reared back looking as though he'd slapped her. Which he pretty much had.

No way he could tell her about Nattat, though, or his desperate, futile attempt to keep her safe. Exerting every ounce of will he possessed, he blanked out the all-too-vivid images of the mountaintop resort in the Caribbean and focused on the woman regarding him with such a bruised look.

"Sorry."

He scraped a hand over his jaw and forced Curaçao to the black pit where it belonged. The clean feel of his chin reminded him that he'd shaved after showering. He must have bristled like a hedgehog when he'd hustled Callie into bed earlier, though. Wincing inwardly, he could only imagine the whisker burns he must have left on her tender skin.

Hell! That was the wrong direction to let his thoughts take him. Exerting an iron will, Joe slammed the door on the image of this woman soft and hot and panting under him.

"Look, Callie, you'll just have to accept there's a big chunk of my past I can't talk about. All that matters is what's between us here and now."

"Funny you should say that. I was actually wondering about that, too." Those purple eyes skewered into him. "What *is* between us, Joe?"

Christ! Where were his alternate escape routes when he needed them? Sweating a little, he reached out. Cupped her chin. Felt a weird lurch under his ribs.

"I can only repeat what I told you earlier. You're a calm port. A safe harbor."

"Right."

She lowered her glance. Her lashes fanned against her cheek, as thick and dark as her shoulder-length hair. Joe had fantasized about that silky mass for the past few weeks. He didn't have to fantasize now. The sight of the dark locks spilling across the pillow had been even more erotic than he'd imagined. It was a sight he intended— hoped!—to enjoy on a regular and frequent basis.

So when she raised her eyes, her calm announcement came down on him like a collapsing brick wall.

"I'm going back to Rome."

"What?"

"Carlo texted me last week." She eased her chin from his hold. "He's offered me a job."

The quiet response triggered a welter of savage reactions. Before agreeing to provide Carlo Luigi Francesco di Lorenzo the high-level personal security his government had requested, Joe and his people had thoroughly researched the prince. The man might be short, balding and getting thick around the middle, but he'd descended from one of the oldest houses in Europe. He also commanded Italy's crack airborne special ops unit.

None of which mattered to Joe at the moment as much as the fact that di Lorenzo had racked up more hours in women's beds than he had hours in the cockpit of his C-130 Hercules.

"Did you know Carlo sits on the board of several charitable foundations?"

Her question brought a curt response.

"Yeah."

Grimacing, Joe raked a hand through his hair and fought to temper both his tone and his visceral reaction to the idea of Callie heading back to Italy on her own. Without Dawn or Kate. Or him.

"Di Lorenzo gave me a list of the organizations he's involved with when I agreed to provide enhanced security," he told her. "Most of his charitable activities are purely economic, but several…"

Joe caught himself. He'd built a reputation and a multimillion-dollar business based on absolute trust. He wouldn't breach a client's confidentiality any more than Callie would the privacy of the children she'd represented in court. Still, he couldn't hold back a terse warning.

"Several of the agencies he's involved with have ties to Africa and the Middle East."

"I know. The job he's offered is with one of those agencies. International Aid to Displaced Women."

Joe felt the tendons in his neck cord. Prince or not, if Carlo thought he could involve Callie in the type of activity he himself had needed protection from, the man had another think coming.

"IADW operates a sort of halfway house for female

refugees," she was explaining. "Women who've escaped or been driven out their own countries and have either lost their male protectors or been abandoned by them somewhere along the way."

"That right? And what does Carlo think you can do for them?"

The question carried more of a bite than he'd intended. So it was no surprise when Callie stiffened.

"Despite the impression I've obviously given you," she said coolly, "I'm neither helpless nor unskilled. At the least, I can help these women acquire a rudimentary English vocabulary, which many of them will need before being resettled in English-speaking countries. At best, perhaps I can ease some of the trauma they've gone through."

Cursing his lack of tact, Joe tried to recover. "Sorry. That came out wrong. What I meant was…"

What he meant was that he didn't like the idea of her working with or for Carlo di Lorenzo. Which was why he committed his second major blunder in as many minutes.

"Look, before you accept his offer, take some time to think about mine."

Her forehead puckered. "Did I miss something? What offer?"

"About coming home. To you."

Her jaw sagged. "Is this…is this a proposal?"

Her surprise knocked him back a step. Hell! He'd thought—been certain—she'd understood where this was going.

"Yes, it's a proposal," he said gruffly. "What'd you think it was?"

"I didn't… That is…" She gave her head a quick, disbelieving shake. "Joe, we barely know each other!"

"Not true."

She'd hit the mark when she'd reminded him that he'd had his people investigate every corner of her life. Joe suspected he'd uncovered a few things about her younger years she wouldn't want her parents to know. He chalked up those early escapades up to her more lively friends, though. Dawn, especially. The voluptuous redhead had started breaking male hearts while still a teenager. Luckily, she seemed to have met her match in Brian Ellis. As Joe had in this dark-haired, violet-eyed siren.

"I've seen your strength and grace under the pressure of threats, Callie. Plus," he added deliberately, "I'd say we got to know each other pretty well this afternoon."

"We certainly did," she agreed, recovering from her astonishment. "And it was wonderful. Off the charts, as Tommy's friend Addy would say."

He waited for the *but* he knew was coming.

"So I hope…I really hope…we can build on that mutual desire."

"With you taking off for Italy?"

"That's where we met," she reminded him, her gaze steady. "Where we can continue to meet. You may not be able to tell me much about your clients, but I gather Carlo's not the first European you've worked with. Nor, I suspect, will he be the last."

She had that right. Joe had put a number of potential clients on hold while he'd tracked the source of Callie's emails. He could pretty well choose the continent, the risk level and the degree of personal involvement in his next contract.

"We could see each other as often in Rome as we could in Boston," she said. "Maybe more often. If you want to make it happen."

Damned if Joe knew at this point.

He'd been so sure she would appreciate what he had to offer. Mutual respect. Sexual compatibility, which they'd more than proved earlier. Financial security. He knew she'd been living on her savings since she'd quit her job. Had thought she'd appreciate that while he wasn't the most expressive or demonstrative man in the world, he was rock solid. Unlike a certain Italian prince.

"I still don't understand. Why go all the way to Rome?"

She chewed on her lower lip. When she answered, Joe sensed she was revealing a part of herself she rarely shared with anyone other than her two friends.

"Your job takes you all over the world. But I grew up, went to school and have worked all my adult life within a ninety-mile radius of Boston. Aside from family vacations and a jaunt to Cancún with Kate and Dawn during one spring break, Italy was my first real adventure. I loved the color, the food, the people. And Rome…!"

A full-blown smile came out, so warm and radiant it slammed into his gut like a rifle butt.

"Oh, Joe! Dawn and Kate and I spent only a few days in Rome. I want more time to explore its rich history and culture. On my own…and with you whenever possible."

Okay. So maybe it wasn't such a bad idea after all. Wandering through the Forum with her. Sharing a bottle of chianti at the tiny trattoria he'd discovered a few blocks from the Spanish Steps. Making love in a hotel room with a view of the old city walls.

They could take the train up to the Lake District for a weekend at some opulent resort. Maybe zip over to Portofino, Italy's answer to the French Riviera. Now that the first shock had passed, Joe could see himself laying all Europe at her feet.

"I guess I can understand where you're coming from," he conceded. "I have one suggestion, though."

"What's that?"

"I think we should…"

He caught himself just in time. Dammit, he had to do this right. Had to appeal to this unexpectedly adventurous side of her personality. And that would necessitate a little more planning and execution on his part.

"I think we should sleep on it," he temporized. "See how we feel in the morning."

A gleam of laughter leaped into her eyes, but she answered with a solemn nod. "By all means, Mr. Russo, let's sleep on it. Your place or mine?"

His DC hotel room was modern and efficient but held none of the comforts of the gatehouse. Callie's smiling invitation to share it with him kicked his pulse into overdrive. It was hammering hard and fast when he tumbled her back onto the sofa cushions.

"Yours, Ms. Langston. Yours."

His internal alarm went off at its usual 5:00 a.m. He came instantly alert but had learned long ago to give no indication he was awake. That skill had saved his life several times, most recently in Curaçao.

Slamming the door on that memory, he kept his eyes closed and concentrated on recording sensory signals. He heard Callie beside him. Her breathy intake, her snuffling exhale. Not quite a snore but close enough to make him smile inwardly. He could feel her, too. Soft and pliant and warm against his side. Her scent filled his nostrils. The lemony tang of her shampoo. The faint, yeasty residue of their lovemaking. One whiff and he felt himself hardening. Only his self-discipline and years of brutal training kept him from rolling her over and burying himself in her hot, tight depths.

He lay quiet, mulling over everything they'd talked about last night. Callie wanted to expand her world. He could understand that. He'd explored damned near every corner of it himself, both in the military and out. Before she went traipsing off to Rome, though, he intended to make sure she wore his brand.

He disciplined himself to wait an hour. It was close to six before he eased out of bed. No sign of the December sun poked through the bedroom shutters as he dragged on his clothes. He needed coffee in the worst way but decided not to wake Callie. Instead, he jotted a quick note and propped it on the kitchen counter.

He hit a Starbucks drive-through and infused the caffeine as he negotiated the still-light traffic in the southeast corner of DC. As early as it was, he knew Frank Harden would be at his desk.

He and Harden had served in Delta Force together before going their separate ways—Joe as a mercenary for some years before starting his own protective services agency, Frank as a civilian analyst with the Defense Intelligence Agency specializing in African affairs. Whip-smart and not shy about voicing his opinion, Harden had progressed steadily up the ranks at the DIA. His current senior executive service rank equated to that of a major general, but neither he nor Joe let that get in the way of the friendship they'd forged all those years ago.

Joe called Harden's private extension when he was almost to the sprawling complex now known as Joint Base Anacostia–Bolling. The base had been formed a few years back by cobbling together the Anacostia Naval Support Facility and Bolling Air Force Base. Since the two installations sat side by side and ate up a big chunk of this corner of DC, Joe guessed the consolidation made sense.

As he'd anticipated, his workaholic pal picked up on the first ring.

"Russo, you mangy dog," Harden drawled in that laconic, down-home Mississippi twang that disguised his needle-sharp instincts and encyclopedic knowledge of all things African. "Where the hell are you, boy?"

"About two blocks away."

"Hot damn! I'll call down to gate B and clear you in."

As promised, Harden got him cleared through the main gate leading to the massive complex that housed DIA headquarters and a slew of other intel activities, like the headquarters of the National Intelligence University and the Joint Functional Component Command for Intelligence, Surveillance and Reconnaissance.

Harden had an underling waiting to escort his guest into the inner sanctum. Joe surrendered the lightweight Ruger LCR-357 that nested in his ankle holster, accepted a signed receipt for it, clipped on a visitors' badge and passed through the metal detector.

Harden's office reflected his exalted pay grade, but Joe had little time to enjoy the view. Rail-thin and every bit as gaunt as the day the two of them had tunneled their way out of a Sudanese prison, the bureaucrat delivered a bone-jarring thump to Joe's shoulder.

"Haven't heard from you since the cows came home. What've you been doin'?"

"Had a job in the Caribbean earlier this year." Joe could feel his insides curl but kept his tone casual. "Most recently at a NATO base north of Venice."

"Yeah, I heard something about that." Frank gestured to one of the armchairs facing his desk. "Rumor is your pal Ellis got a fat contract out of that gig. Some new avionics package for the entire NATO airlift fleet."

"Could be."

Joe knew damn well it was more than a rumor. He'd gotten to know Brian Ellis well during that NATO gig and at his request had recently completed a top-to-bottom scrub of his company's physical, industrial and cyber security. What had begun as a business association, however, had morphed into friendship.

"So what can I do you for?" Frank asked. "Or did you just come to gloat 'bout me being chained to a desk?"

"I need some info."

"Figured. Shoot."

"What can you tell me about a Rome-based charity called International Aid to Displaced Women?"

Joe left the Defense Intelligence Agency feeling marginally better about Callie's decision. Although Frank wasn't personally familiar with IADW, he had his people run a quick screen.

He also made a call to a contact at the State Department responsible for overseeing the US Refugee Admissions Program and the 6 billion dollars provided through the combined efforts of the Bureau of Population, Refugees and Migration and the US Agency for International Development. The contact's people in turn worked closely with a host of other agencies, including the Office of the UN High Commissioner for Refugees, the UN World Food Programme, the International Red Cross, the UN Children's Fund and the International Organization for Migration. Most of these organizations had special programs in place to protect the most vulnerable sectors of the population, including women and girls.

Harden's contact had verified that the Rome operation was legit. Equally important, there'd been no documented reports of terrorists or hard-core criminals infiltrating the population the agency cared for. That wasn't to say they couldn't. Given the growing number of women being recruited by groups like ISIS, the PLF and Sri Lanka's Tamil Tigers, programs that helped women enter or re-settle in other countries made tempting conduits.

Joe intended to go over the agency's refugee screening process with Carlo in some detail before Callie started work there. He made a quick call to his twenty-four-hour operations center and instructed the on-duty controller to check on an evening flight. The controller clicked a few keys and said there was a flight leaving Dulles at 5:40 p.m. Joe would have to hump to get everything done and be at the airport the required three hours early for international flights, but he figured he could make it.

"Okay, book it."

He then contacted the office of the director of the Na-ples film festival. Marcello Audi was worried that allow-ing a certain entry to be shown at this year's festival would put them on radical jihadists' hit list. He'd requested a thorough security assessment of all venues. Joe had planned to pass on the job, but Callie's little bombshell last night had triggered a swift reordering of his schedule. The Naples job would only take a few weeks, and it would put him less than an hour south of Rome. After that...

After that, he promised himself, he and Callie would settle on a permanent arrangement. One that gave them *both* a safe, comfortable haven. With that goal in mind, he steered his rental to the next stop on his hastily con-structed agenda.

Chapter Four

Callie sat curled up on the sitting room sofa, wearing loose, comfortable sweats and fuzzy slippers on her feet. She had fresh coffee in a Christmas mug and her iPhone within reach. She'd slept late—hardly a surprise given last night's strenuous exercise—and woken to find Joe gone. When she'd wandered into the kitchen, she found his note asking her to hold off calling Carlo until he got back.

She hoped he wasn't going to try to talk her out of Rome. He'd seemed to accept her decision last night, even admitted that he could see just as much of her in Italy as in Boston. She really wanted to contact Carlo and tell him she was accepting his job offer.

She itched to tell Kate and Dawn, too. And not just about Rome. There was this whole exciting, surprising, confusing matter of a proposal to share. They'd both already texted asking a) if she was awake b) if Joe was still there and c) whether she'd resolved the Lassie issue. She wanted to go over to the main house, huddle with Dawn so they could FaceTime Kate together. The three of them had shared so many secrets, so many of life's ups and downs. But Joe's note had asked her to wait, so she'd held off, prey to a slightly disconcerting tug of divided loyalties.

She was still feeling the tug when she heard a car pull into the drive. A quick glance through the front windows confirmed Joe's return. Uncurling, she was halfway down the hall before the bell rang. When she opened the door, he walked in looking every bit as tall and strong as he had when he arrived from Sydney yesterday, but *so* much sexier. Which, of course, might have something to do with the fact that she'd explored every flat plane and hard ridge of the body that went with his steel-gray eyes and square chin.

God! Was she totally insane? What woman in her right mind wouldn't jump at Joe's offer? Why *not* settle into a comfortable nest with him? Why *not* be there, waiting patiently, when he rolled in from one of his unspecified, no-questions-allowed assignments?

When he greeted her with a quick kiss and one of his rare smiles, her uncharacteristic self-doubt spiked again. But before she could give in to the sudden urge to tell him she was reconsidering her options, he preempted her with a brusque announcement.

"I talked to a buddy at the Defense Intelligence Agency. The International Aid to Displaced Women operation's legit."

"Good to know. Although…" She lifted a brow. "Did you think Carlo would invite me to work for an organization that wasn't?"

"Doesn't hurt to check."

"No, I guess not. Aren't you staying?" she asked when he made no move to shed his bomber jacket.

"Can't. Have some things to get done before I fly out this afternoon."

"Fly where?"

She'd blurted it out without thinking and half expected another rebuff. This time, however, Joe provided details.

"First to Rome. I told Carlo I want to review IADW's refugee screening process before you arrive. Then to Naples. I'll be doing some work—"

"Wait! Back up." She couldn't believe what she'd just heard. "You told Carlo that I was coming to Rome? To work at IADW?"

He blinked, as surprised by her sharp tone as she'd been by his abrupt announcement a few moments ago. "You said last night that's what you wanted. Did you change your mind?"

"No." A surge of irritation smothered her earlier doubts. "I would, however, have appreciated the opportunity to tell my prospective employer *personally* that I'd accepted his generous job offer."

"Oh. Yeah. Sorry." He scraped a palm across his chin. "It's just…"

"Yes?"

"You've seen the news coverage. The attacks in France and Belgium and other parts of the world. Some of those terrorists got into place by posing as refugees and entering through legitimate refugee resettlement conduits. I just want to make sure IADW isn't one of them."

Her irritation melted. A little. Even more when he brushed a knuckle down her cheek. His touch was warm. Soothing. Possessive.

"Keeping you safe's becoming my number-one priority, Pansy Eyes."

She had to smile at the endearment. And she could hardly argue with his desire to protect her. Not after she'd burrowed in this admittedly luxurious hole while he tracked down the creep who'd sent the emails. Yet the little corner of her mind that rejected the prospect of being wrapped in cotton wool for the rest of her life reared its nasty head again.

"Thank you, Joe."

She meant that. She really did. Still, she took a small, instinctive step back when he extracted a small jeweler's box out of his coat pocket.

"I know this is pushing things, Callie, but I saw this before I flew to Australia and asked them to hold it. I wanted you to check it out, see if you liked it. Now, with this Rome deal, I figured I'd take a chance."

"Joe…"

"It's not as flashy or sparkly as some I looked at," he said, flipping up the lid, "but it's almost the same color as your eyes. And the setting is kind of nice."

More than nice, Callie saw on a little intake of breath. It was exquisite. White gold, she guessed, spun into a filigree bouquet to showcase a gleaming oval amethyst. The end prongs were long-stemmed roses, the side prongs delicate leaves with a tiny dove nested between them.

"Joe, I…"

She floundered, tugged in a dozen different directions by the whirlwind of emotions this man roused in her. He noted her confusion with a small smile and pounced.

"It doesn't have to mean anything more than you want it to, Callie. Here, try it on for size." He slid it over her knuckle. "Good. It fits. I wanted you to have it before you took off for Rome."

She glanced up from the glowing amethyst and caught the glint of male satisfaction in his eyes.

"And," she guessed drily, "you wanted me to be wearing it when I meet with Carlo."

"Yeah, that, too."

The admission was totally unapologetic and so...so *Joe* that she had to smile.

"I like Carlo as a friend and now a prospective employer," she said. "That's all. Surely you know that."

"Of course I do. Doesn't hurt to reinforce the message, though." His gaze held hers, steady and unflinching. "You change your mind, or want to send a different signal after you get to Rome, just take it off. I'll understand."

Callie debated for some moments after Joe left. Her first instinct was to scurry next door, corner Dawn in her spacious home office and get Kate on FaceTime. A glance at the clock brought a swift revision to that plan. It was close to eleven o'clock, and her news was too momentous to share electronically. Two quick calls set up an emergency girls-only luncheon at an upscale eatery only a block from the thirteen-story high-rise on G Street where Kate worked.

Rushing into the bedroom, Callie exchanged her sweats and fuzzy slippers for boots, slacks and a roll-neck sweater. She angled a black angora beret sideways to keep her head warm and bundled up in a paisley scarf, gloves and the ankle-length khaki duster she'd snagged during a sale at Nordstrom.

She met a similarly muffled and extremely curious

Dawn on the flagstone walk connecting the main house to the guesthouse.

"What's the emergency?"

"I'll tell you and Kate together. You drive. You know your way around better than I do."

The light snow of the day before had pretty much turned to mush, but holiday decorations added bright touches of red, gold and green as Dawn negotiated DC's always busy streets. When she pulled up at the popular bistro and turned her Mustang over to the valet, the two women hurried inside.

It was still early, not yet eleven thirty, so Kate had been able to snag a booth by the round fireplace in the center of the restaurant. The noise level was still low enough for Nat King Cole's velvet-voiced rendition of "The Christmas Song" to provide the perfect complement to the crackle of flames.

Her tawny hair caught up in a smooth twist, Kate looked every inch the professional in a ruby blazer that hid her almost baby bump, white blouse and a flowing black skirt that draped over the top of her boots. She laid aside the menu she'd been examining and looked up expectantly as Callie and Dawn shed their outdoor gear before sliding into the booth.

"Okay, Miss Priss and Boots. What's so important that…oh, my God!" Jaw dropping, Kate grabbed the hand Callie was using to shake out her napkin. "This is *gorgeous*!"

Beside her Dawn gasped in surprise. "You stinker! Is that what I think it is?"

"Sort of."

"Sort of?" Kate angled Callie's hand from side to side. "What does that mean? Did you and Joe settle the Lassie question or not?"

"Not exactly. But we're working on it."

A server decked out in a sparkly red bow tie approached. Dawn waved him off with a quick smile.

"Give us a few minutes. We're talking some serious girl stuff here." She slewed around again. "Back to you and Joe and that hunk of quartz you're sporting. What's the bottom line?"

"The bottom line? Okay, brace yourself. I'm taking Carlo up on his offer of a job at International Aid to Displaced Women, and Joe wants me wearing his brand when I fly over to Rome on Thursday."

Her friends reacted with equal parts surprise and dismay.

"You're going to Rome?"

"This *Thursday*?" Dawn wailed. "You can't go this Thursday! Christmas is less than two weeks away. The three of us have gathered at one or the other's house every Christmas since, when? Fifth grade?"

"You've got Brian and Tommy to share it with now. And Kate and Travis. You'll have a house full."

"It won't be the same," she said stubbornly. "Wonderful, but not the same."

"The position I'll be filling has been vacant for several months," Callie explained. "The director—my new boss—is anxious to get someone in place."

"We're only talking another few weeks," Kate protested. "Surely your boss can wait until after the holidays."

"Evidently not." A small smile played at the corners of Callie's mouth. "From what I can gather based on my brief conversation with Carlo this morning, he's a bit intimidated by the woman."

Her friends shared another astonished look. Neither Kate nor Dawn could envision any mere female intimidating Carlo di Lorenzo. The cocky Italian Special Forces pilot with the string of royal titles after his name had racked up hundreds of combat hours. According to the paparazzi, he'd also charmed his way in and out of the same number of bedrooms.

"This director must be a real witch," Kate warned. "You sure you want to work for someone like that?"

"I'll be in Italy," Callie said softly. "Remember what happened to you there? And to you, Dawn?"

That silenced the other women for a few moments. Kate went all dewy eyed thinking of the surprise ceremony Travis had arranged at the Trevi Fountain to renew their wedding vows. Dawn could only grin at the memory of the sparks she and Brian had struck off each other when they'd met in Venice. She came out of her reverie in time to wave the waiter away again.

"What about Joe?" Kate asked. "He's content to let you zip off to Rome as long as you're wearing his ring?"

Callie gave a small huff. "Not hardly. By the time he got around to slipping it on my finger this morning, he'd already contacted a pal in the Defense Intelligence Agency and had them check out the organization I'll be working for. Then he told Carlo that he's flying in tonight to do a scrub of the center's screening procedures. And he set up a job for himself in Naples."

"Naples is only an hour south of Rome."

Kate should know. She'd researched train schedules and driving times and every possible tourist sight for their trip to Italy a few months back.

"So Joe informed me." Callie fingered the ring again. "He also informed me that all I have to do is take this off and he'll drop out of the picture, no harm, no foul."

"Oh, that's romantic," Dawn snorted. "Please tell me he didn't use those actual words."

"Pretty close."

"Well? Are you going to remove it?"

"No." Sighing, Callie shook her head. "Not now, anyway. I'm still trying to sort out how I feel about him."

"How *do* you feel? Right this exact second."

"Happy. Confused. Excited. And," she admitted with a reluctant laugh, "completely in lust."

Neither of her friends could argue with that. Or talk her out of relocating to Italy. Resigning themselves to the inevitable, they helped Callie tie up the loose ends she'd left dangling when she'd taken refuge in the Ellises' gatehouse.

"I'll zip up to Boston," Dawn volunteered. "I can sort through your closet and send you what you'll need in Rome. But what do you want me to do with rest of it? Your furniture, your houseplants, your ton and a half of books?"

"The books and furniture will have to go in storage. I'm pretty sure Mrs. Eckstein, my neighbor, will take the plants."

"How about your lease?" the fiscally minded Kate asked. "Does it allow you to sublet?"

"The lease is actually up for renewal at the end of next month. Since I'm not giving them the required sixty days' notice, I'll probably have to forfeit January's rent and my security deposit."

"Let me handle that. As for Rome, you shouldn't have any trouble using your credit card for purchases or withdrawing cash at an ATM. But you should open an account at a local branch and transfer some operating funds, just in case. I'll get the paperwork started, if you want."

"Thank you. Thank both of you!"

The gratitude came straight from Callie's heart. Yet

she had to suppress a stupid little twinge at how easy it was to cut all ties to the life she'd lived in Boston for six years.

Oh, for…! What was her problem? This was what she wanted. What she'd wished for at the Trevi Fountain! Adventure. Romance. A whole new chapter in her life.

"Won't you need a license to practice in Italy?" Dawn asked, still working the logistics in her mind.

"I would, if I was working in an Italian treatment facility or setting up my own practice. That's not the case here. The IADW center is physically located in Rome, but it's governed by an international body with different credentialing requirements. According to their standards, I'm actually *over*qualified for the work I'll be doing."

"And your parents?" Kate put in. "Have you told them you're zipping off to Europe?"

"Not yet. I wanted you guys to be the first to know. I'll call them after lunch."

They'd be surprised, Callie knew, but not particularly concerned. Since moving to a seniors-only retirement village in central Florida six years ago, her retired teacher mom and former postal worker dad had become totally immersed in new hobbies and activities. Including, she remembered with an inner smile, their latest passion for bird-watching. She hadn't told them about the vicious emails, and they'd voiced only mild curiosity about her extended stay in DC.

"So you're really going to do it," Dawn said, breaking into her thoughts.

"I am."

"In that case we need to celebrate with our favorite Italian drink." A smile and an uplifted finger brought the patient server to the table. "We want three Bellinis—two regular and one virgin for the pregnant lady."

The young server looked confused. "I don't know if there is such a thing as a virgin Bellini."

"Tell the barkeep to improvise," Dawn instructed airily.

Despite her friends' wish that she would wait until after the holidays, Callie stuck to her decision to report to her new job the following Monday. She flew out of Dulles late Thursday afternoon and thoroughly enjoyed the unexpected and unaccustomed luxury of an upgrade to business class compliments of Joe. When she landed at Rome's Leonardo da Vinci Airport early Friday morning, she zinged off a text to let Kate and Dawn know she'd arrived.

She cleared customs with the intention of spending the day setting up the small flat that came with her new job and the weekend exploring the neighborhood around it. She hadn't included Joe Russo in her plans, however. Looking like Italy's answer to Patrick Dempsey in snug jeans, a black turtleneck and his tan bomber jacket, he met her in the arrivals terminal and welcomed her with a hard, hot kiss. She was still recovering from that when his take-charge personality emerged.

"Are you totally wiped?" he asked as he steered her to the baggage claim area.

"Not wiped at all. I slept most of the flight in lie-flat leather luxury." She hesitated, but innate honesty made her ask. "I saw that the upgrade was charged to JLR Security. It won't be billed as a business expense, will it? If so, I'll reimburse you."

He glanced down at her, amusement flickering in those stone-gray eyes. "Not to worry. I use a top-fifty accounting firm. They keep my personal and professional accounts straight."

"Good to know. Except I'm used to paying my own way. I don't expect—or want—you to pick up the tab every time we're together."

"Well, we shouldn't have many expenses in Naples this weekend. I'm meeting with my prospective client, so my time will be charged to him."

"Naples? I can't go to Naples this weekend! I've got too much to do here in Rome."

"You might want to reconsider. Today's the feast of Santa Lucia. I'm told her day sort of officially kicks off the Christmas season. Marcello—my prospective client—has invited us to join him and his family for their traditional dinner tonight. It would give me a chance to get to know him in an informal setting, assess what kind of man he is."

"But…"

The rumble of the baggage conveyor belt cut off her protest. By the time Joe had snagged her two suitcases, she'd reassessed her priorities. From the sound of it, this meeting was important to Joe. Unpacking and settling into the apartment could wait.

Or not. To her surprise, he'd planned for that, too. After asking if she needed anything other than her roll-on for the weekend trip, he turned her bags over to the associate waiting beside a slick black SUV.

"This is Emilio Mancera, head of my operations here in Italy."

"Ciao, Emilio."

"Ciao, signorina. *Benvenuto a Roma.*"

Dark eyed, curly haired and the possessor of a proud Roman nose to go with the muscles that bulged under his fleece pullover, the thirtysomething Italian loaded the bags in the SUV.

"I will take these to your apartment, *sì*? And make sure the kitchen contains all you need."

"I, uh, *sì. Grazie.*"

He conducted a brief exchange with Joe in swift Italian before giving Callie another cheerful ciao and departing.

She glanced at Joe while he beeped the locks on a second SUV in the adjoining space. Why hadn't she picked up on the fact that he spoke the language when she'd first met him here in Italy? It was just one more gap in her knowledge about this man and his past. Gaps she intended to bridge. Starting now, she decided after they'd left the parking garage and hit the bright, brittle December sunlight.

"You sounded pretty fluent in that exchange with Emilio. Where did you learn Italian?"

"Here and there. My five-month gig with Carlo considerably expanded my vocabulary. Although," he added with a sardonic tilt to his head, "most of it can't be repeated in polite company."

"Do you speak any other languages?"

"Some Spanish. A little French. Enough Portuguese to ask directions to the closest bar."

"Portuguese? I'm impressed."

Shrugging, he aimed for the airport exit. "You take a job in Angola, it helps to be able to communicate with the local cops."

Callie tried to sketch a mental image of Africa. She knew Angola was near the continent's southern tip but couldn't place it on the east or west coast.

"What did you do there?"

He shot her a quick glance. Callie kicked herself, thinking she'd crossed the line again. She was suppressing a twinge of resentment at being shut out of his past when he decided to let her in a bare inch or two.

"How much do you know about Angola?"

"Nothing, I'm embarrassed to admit."

"It sits on huge mineral and petroleum reserves, and its economy is among the fastest growing in the world. Problem is, a handful of wealthy elites control the economy."

"Which makes them prime targets," Callie guessed.

"Exactly."

Okay, he'd cracked the door. She pushed it just a little harder.

"Your client was one of these incredibly wealthy elites?"

His expression didn't change but Callie could sense him drawing into himself. Again.

"Dammit, Joe. You brought up the job in Angola. You can't just leave me hanging. Yes or no? Was your client one of these wealthy elites?"

"No."

Well, she'd set herself up for that one. She was about to let the grudging remark go when he surprised her with a terse follow-up.

"She was at the other end of the spectrum," he said, his jaw tight. "A young, passionate member of parliament who wanted to curb the elites' power. My team and I smuggled her out of the country the day before her appointment with a firing squad."

"Good grief! Where is she now?"

"Dead."

The single syllable hit like a glass of ice water to the face. When Callie recoiled against her seat back, Joe wrenched his gaze from the road.

"An assassin got to her in Curaçao." His tone was as cold as his eyes. "And I got to him."

Her breath stuck in her throat. She had to swallow twice before she got out a quavering, "Good."

As shaky as it was, her endorsement seemed to pull Joe from the dark cave of his memories. The taut angle of his jaw eased. So did the tension cording his neck above his jacket collar.

"Helluva a way to kick off what I'd planned as a fun weekend," he growled.

Still startled by the piece of his past she'd pried loose, Callie forced a smile. "I'm sure it'll be fun. How could a traditional Italian family dinner be anything but?"

Blessedly ignorant of the noisy, exuberant, exhausting evening ahead, she relaxed in her seat and vowed to keep the conversation away from dark subjects as they hit the autostrada and rolled south.

Chapter Five

Since Joe's client didn't expect them until late afternoon, they made the drive down from Rome in leisurely stages.

They stopped first at the Abbey of Monte Cassino. Perched atop a steep precipice overlooking the main road to Rome, the abbey had become a key objective in the Allies' push north during WWII. Their efforts to dislodge the Germans resulted in a murderous battle than caused more than 190,000 casualties and left the abbey and town at its base in smoking ruins. Rebuilt after the war, Monte Cassino now offered visitors a glimpse of its original medieval glory. The grim history of the battle and accompanying artifacts interested Joe, of course, but Callie delighted in the priceless manuscripts and religious treasures that had been taken to Rome for safekeeping and returned to the abbey after the war.

Closer to Naples, the warm Mediterranean currents

chased the chill from the air, and the temperature rose. Callie wiggled out of her wool duster and tossed it in the backseat. Joe did the same with his leather jacket. When they left the autostrada for lunch at a trattoria recommended by Joe's prospective client, they opted to sit outside on a vine-draped patio. The setting was idyllic but it was the cloud-wrapped mountain in the distance that held Callie's fascinated gaze.

"Is that Vesuvius?"

"Looks like it."

"Do we have time to visit the ruins of Pompeii?"

"Not if you want to do them justice. Maybe tomorrow. Or Sunday, before we head back to Rome."

Not quite believing that she was actually here, in the shadow of Mount Vesuvius, she took the friendly server's recommendation and ordered a local specialty of sausage served with broccoli rabe. Joe went the more traditional route of pasta in a red sauce, with meatballs served separately as the second course.

Feeling deliciously lazy afterward, she expected them to head into Naples. Instead Joe skirted the city's sprawling outskirts.

"Signor Audi lives in the city," he explained, "but his family's ancestral farm is another forty-five minutes south. Or more correctly, their ancestral ranch."

"They raise cattle?"

"Water buffalo. They've got about three hundred head on their ranch."

"What in the world do they do with... Oh! They make mozzarella?"

"The best in Italy, according to Signor Audi."

Despite her extensive reading, Callie couldn't imagine how the big, plodding, wide-horned water buffalo had migrated to Italy. From Asia, probably, herded across the Mongolian steppes by nomadic tribes. Or maybe imported by the Arabs who'd invaded Sicily. But there was no denying mozzarella had pretty much become associated with all things Italian.

Still, she wasn't prepared for Campania's rich grasslands. Wide, rolling pastures bordered the road and stretched all the way to the sea that could be glimpsed through tall, thin cypresses and silver-barked eucalyptus trees. Dotting these pastures were herds of black buffalo grazing placidly or wallowing contentedly in man-made ponds with sloping ramps. The air wafting through the SUV's vents carried a mix of grass and salt sea air, along with an earthy hint of dung.

When the navigational system pinged a few minutes later, Joe turned left and drove through a pair of stone pillars. A cypress-lined road led them past more fenced pastures and ended in a broad yard bordered on one side by a long, narrow building with huge roller brushes at its entrance.

"Is that a car wash?" Callie asked in surprise.

Joe's glance flicked from the brushes to the gleaming stainless steel tank truck parked at the building's far end. "I'm guessing that's the barn where they milk the buffalo. They probably have to scrub 'em down first to make sure the milk stays clean."

Her mind boggled at the thought of one of those huge buffalo going through a series of washes and waxes like the family car. Trying to visualize the process, she looked around the rest of the yard with some interest. Older buildings and sheds constructed of local stone housed tractors and various other pieces of farm equipment.

A rambling, two-story residence sat a little farther down the road. Surrounded by ancient cypresses that stood tall and spear straight, its varying levels suggested it had been added to numerous times over the years. Like the other buildings, it, too, was constructed of stone covered almost entirely with a pale yellow plaster. U-shaped terra cotta tiles delineated the varying roof lines, and bright green shutters framed its many windows. Flowers spilled from window boxes, stone urns, even the wooden bucket dangling over what must have once been a working well.

Adding to the color were the scattered children's toys…a red-and-blue plastic Big Wheel, a hot pink bike with training wheels and sparkly handlebar streamers, a forgotten doll with the pale hair and blue gown of Princess Elsa from *Frozen*.

Callie was thinking of all the times she'd watched that particular video with Tommy when two dogs raced from behind the house and offered a raucous greeting. One was a mottled gray and black of an indeterminate breed, the other a small collie. They were noisy but not vicious, as evidenced by the greeting they gave Joe after he exited the SUV and squatted to let them sniff his hand.

Callie climbed out as well and breathed in the pungent tang of a working farm overlaid with the perfume of so many flowers. She was letting the dogs scope her out when a woman strode out of the house. In boots, tight jeans and a loose-knit sweater, she moved with the careless, casual grace that seemed as natural as breathing to so many Italian women.

"Signor Russo, Signorina Langston, welcome. I am Arianna Audi de Luca." Her dark eyes were friendly, her handshake firm. "My father apologizes that he is not here to greet you. He and my husband are at the barn. One of our buffalo has gone into the milking chamber and does not wish to come out. She can be very stubborn, that Domenica, but she'll usually come to Papà when he whistles to her."

"Domenica? Is that her breed?"

"No, no, it is her name."

Callie's glance swept past her to the hulking black animals in the pasture. "You name them all?"

"Not all. But this one is like a pet, yes? When she was but a tiny calf, she followed my brother and me everywhere." Head cocked, Arianna issued a smiling invitation. "If you're not too tired from your journey, perhaps you would like to meet her? And see something of the milking process?"

Callie wasn't about to pass up the chance to see the cow wash in operation. "I'd like that."

Joe seconded the idea, and their hostess gave them a quick history as she led them back toward the barn. With each step the scents of fresh-cut grass and dung edged out the flowers a little more.

"With Papà and my brother so busy in Naples, my husband and I manage the farm. It's been in our family since the sixteenth century. We have a framed copy of the original deed in the office."

Her expression turned serious.

"There are many cruelties in this business, but my family has spent much time and money over the years to make ours humane. As you'll see, we use the voluntary milking method. We also hold to the strict sanitary standards required for DOP certification. *Scusi*. DOP stands for *denominazione di origine protetta*. It means our mozzarella meets the highest government standards for quality and excellence."

Angling to the left, she pointed out a wide metal chute that led from the pasture to the giant roller brushes. Several large bovines waited patiently in the chute while others milled near its mouth.

"The females come when they wish to be milked. Since it is all done by machine, they do not have to follow a set schedule. They enter here and…"

The sudden rumble of an engine starting and gears engaging interrupted her.

"Ah! Papà has convinced Domenica to leave the milking chamber. Now the others may enter. But first they take a little bath, yes?"

Streams of water arced across the barn entrance, the giant rollers whirred into action and the lead buffalo in the chute ambled up the low ramp. Tail swishing, it disappeared into the mist.

"Amazing," Callie murmured. "They're not afraid of it at all."

"I think they consider it a spa treatment," Arianna replied, laughing. "We give them jets of cool water in the heat of summer, warm water in winter."

Dodging the spray, she ushered them through a side door and into a spacious work area. "This is the office, where my husband takes care of all the necessary forms and endless paperwork. And here…"

She opened another door to show a small room with stainless steel counters and an impressive array of laboratory equipment.

"Here is where I spend much of my time."

Callie could see why. A quick glance at the framed degrees on the wall beside the door indicted Arianna Maria Patrizia Audi had earned a bachelor of science in organic chemistry from Stanford and a *laurea magistrale* in *biotecnologia agricola* from the University of Pisa.

"I'm working to increase the conjugated linoleic acid

content in our herd's milk," she informed them. "There's some evidence it possesses anticancer properties. It may also affect insulin response. Sadly, the science is not there yet. One can only keep researching."

After the high-powered cow wash and pristine lab, Callie wasn't surprised to see the single worker in the milking area wearing immaculate white coveralls, a hairnet and plastic booties over his shoes. He didn't appear to have much of a job, however. Just stood by as the newly scrubbed buffalo meandered into a narrow chamber. A second later, a robotic arm slid under her. The animal got another wash, this one from a gentle upspray, then six flexible tubes snaked upward. Like cobras, they curled and wove and latched onto their prey.

"Good grief!" Astonished, Callie watched for some reaction from the buffalo, but she didn't so much as blink her long, curling lashes. "How did those cups magically attach to her udder?"

"They're equipped with optical cameras and lasers that detect the exact position of each teat. Once attached, the cup will rinse the teat again with warm water and gently massage it to stimulate the premilk. That gets flushed into a side line, then the rest will flow through the main milking line and empty directly into the truck you see outside for transport to our plant in town."

"No wonder Domenica didn't want to leave the chamber," Callie couldn't help commenting. "She must really enjoy all that flushing and massaging."

"She does," Arianna confirmed with a laugh. "What female would not?"

Both women glanced at Joe. He merely lifted his brows, but to Callie's surprise and secret amusement a faint tinge of red crept into his cheeks.

Would she ever understand this man? Only this morning he'd admitted taking out an assassin, and now here he was, embarrassed to hear two women discussing udders and teats. Smothering a grin, she listened as their guide continued.

"Once the milk stops flowing, the cups disengage and the udders are washed again, then sprayed with disinfectant."

They followed the chamber's current occupant toward the exit. The buffalo entered another chute that led to the pasture, and Arianna and her guests emerged into the yard.

"That was *so* interesting," Callie said. "I had no idea cattle milking had become so mechanized."

"Not all farms are as progressive as ours. And there… Ah! Here is Papà."

Callie's first, startled thought was that the gentleman who hurried toward them looked just like Rossano Brazzi, the hunky Italian actor who'd starred alongside Louis Jourdan in *Three Coins in the Fountain*. Tall, tanned, wavy haired and full lipped, he greeted Joe with a hearty handshake and Callie with a traditional kiss to both cheeks.

"I'm so pleased you could join us, Signorina Langston. I see Arianna has been showing you a little of what makes our mozzarella the best in Campania."

"She has, and I must say I'm very impressed."

"You will be even more so once you taste it. Please, let us escort you to the house and introduce you to the rest of the family."

Four hours, two dozen or so relatives, several glasses of wine, a ginormous platter of pasta and six different flavors of mozzarella later, Signor Audi asked his daughter to entertain Callie while he took Joe into his study for a private discussion. Not that she needed entertaining. She was so stuffed she could barely move. She was also beginning to feel jet lag creeping up on her. Comfortably ensconced on the sofa, she was more than content to listen with half an ear to the buzz of conversation conducted mostly in Italian and watch Arianna's two young children setting candles into ornate ceramic holders to be lit in honor of Saint Lucia.

"It's a tradition for us," their mother explained, her feet up and her ankles crossed on a hassock. "One that dates back almost a thousand years. Lucia means light, yes? She was martyred on this day in December, which under the Julian calendar was then the winter solstice."

"The shortest day of the year," Callie commented.

"Exactly! So for us the lighting of candles signals the end of the dark winter as well as the beginning of the twelve days of Christmas. When we light the candles, we sing her song and give the children sweets and small gifts."

"'Santa Lucia.' I know that song."

She should. The famous Neapolitan hymn had been recorded by everyone from opera greats like Enrico Caruso and Luciano Pavarotti to modern-day classical crossover star Hayley Westenra. Even Elvis Presley had sung it in one of his most popular movies, *Viva Las Vegas*. Movie buffs that they were, Callie, Kate and Dawn had watched the classic starring Elvis and Ann-Margret a half dozen times.

"You have another interesting Christmas tradition."

Callie nodded to the A-frame crèche that occupied an entire corner of the room. It was the largest and most elaborate she'd ever seen. Five, maybe six feet tall, it contained several tiers of shelves filled with wrapped gifts, fragrant pine boughs, small candles and far more figures than she was used to seeing in a Christmas nativity scene. Some of the exquisitely detailed and gorgeously painted figurines wore the simple robes of shepherds and goat herders. Others were garbed in what looked like costumes from a dozen different historical eras, including modern-day soccer garb.

"I've never seen soccer players in a manger scene before."

"That, too, is very Neapolitan," Arianna told her. "We add new figures to our crèche every year, and the new addition doesn't always have biblical significance. It could be a famous person from the past, a great opera star, even a president or politician." Grinning, she pointed to a figure in modern clothing. "Do you see that grim gentleman there, on the far right? That's our current prime minister. Papà added him this year. He feels the poor, misguided soul needs as much heavenly exposure as he can get."

"We have a few politicians in the States who could use more, too."

"You would probably see many familiar figures for sale on Via San Gregorio Armeno. That's where the artisans who make the cribs display their wares. You *must* stroll down that street while you're in Naples. You'll see nothing else like it in the world."

"I'll certainly check it out if I have time before we head back to Rome."

"Ah, yes. Papà tells me you are to work with Carlo di Lorenzo." Her voice took on a cautious note. "You've met him before?"

"Several times."

"*Bene.* Then you know to expect the most extravagant offers to jet away with him to Casablanca or Hong Kong."

"His last offer was Dubai," Callie confirmed.

"And Joe?" Arianna asked curiously. "He knows this about Carlo?"

"He does."

Callie didn't realize she was fingering her ring until it drew the other woman's gaze.

"That amethyst is gorgeous, and the setting so unusual."

"Thank you. I'm still not quite used to it."

"I begin to understand." Arianna's dark eyes danced. "If Joe Russo gave you that beautiful ring, not even Carlo di Lorenzo can mistake its message. Whether he will choose to heed it, however, is another matter altogether."

"Sounds like you know the prince pretty well."

"I, too, have been invited to fly away with him. But," she added on a merry laugh, "that was before I settled down with a husband, two bambini and three hundred water buffalo."

When Joe and Signor Audi returned, Callie confessed she was starting to feel the combined effects of her long flight, the delicious dinner and several glasses of wine. They made their farewells a few moments later and left with invitations to visit again, an exchange of phone numbers and a promise from Arianna to call Callie the next time she was in Rome. They must do lunch, the buffalo rancher declared, and shop at some of the city's elegant little boutiques.

"I hope she does call," Callie said as she settled in the soft leather seat. "It would be nice to hit the shops with a friend."

She wanted to stay awake for the short drive into Naples. She would really like to experience the city for the first time bathed in moonlight. She was also eager to see the colorful Christmas lights Arianna said were strung from building to building in alleys so narrow that second- and third-story residents could almost shake hands with neighbors living across the street.

She remembered clicking her seat belt. Remembered her head lolling against the back rest. The next thing she knew Joe had opened the passenger side door and was unclicking her belt.

"Whrarwe?"

"At the hotel. C'mon, sweetheart, let's get you to bed."

The parking valet took the SUV, and Joe took her arm. While he checked them in, Callie registered sleepy impressions of a lobby with more marble than the pyramids of Giza, a wide circular staircase draped with exquisitely decorated garlands and a Christmas tree that soared three or four stories.

Once in their suite, her jet lag hit with a vengeance. Close to comatose, she left a trail of clothes from a sitting room graced by a massive sofa to a bedroom dominated by a four-poster bed draped with shimmering, champagne-colored silk. In bra and panties, she crawled under the covers. A sleep-starved corner of her mind registered the small thud of Joe placing their carryalls on the bench at the foot of the bed. The faint whisper as he undressed. The dip of the mattress when he slid in and pulled her against him. His chest was warm against her back, his thighs hard under her butt. With a sound halfway between a sigh and a whimper, she snuggled closer and sank into oblivion.

She woke to thin shafts of sunlight sneaking through the drapes and hazy realization she was still spooned against Joe. She smiled in perfect contentment and went back to sleep.

It could have been moments or hours before she blinked awake again. Pushing up on one elbow, she discovered the other half of the bed was empty and the covers neatly smoothed. The only sound disturbing the stillness was the faint honk of a car horn outside the draped windows.

"Joe?"

No answer from either the bathroom or the spacious sitting room visible through open double doors. Tossing back the covers, Callie padded to the bath. Each step brought the delicious sensation of her feet sinking into inch-thick silk carpet. The room itself stopped her in her tracks.

The decadent bath was a symphony in marble—gleaming black-and-white squares on the floors, dove-gray patterned with what looked like real gold swirls on the walls, a matching slab of gold-toned stone on the countertops. The walk-in shower was as large as the kitchen in her Boston apartment, and the claw-foot tub sat in regal splendor on a raised dais.

Good grief! This hotel suite must cost a fortune. She felt an uneasy twinge thinking back to yesterday, when she'd insisted on paying her share of expenses. Then she remembered Joe saying his prospective client would pick up the tab. The mozzarella business must be booming.

Joe's business, too, if he catered to such super-wealthy clients. He and Callie had never discussed either the size or the financial base of his company. They'd had no reason to. Just one more aspect of the Joe Russo enigma she knew nothing about.

Thinking of the gaps in their knowledge of each

other, she padded to the shell-shaped sink with its gold faucets and arching swan's neck spigots. None of the fixtures showed a single water spot despite the obvious signs Joe had used them earlier—his razor, shaving cream and aftershave were lined up in precise order beside a leather shaving kit. He'd even folded back the top sheet of toilet paper, she noted with some amusement.

Her immediate needs attended to, she snuggled into one the hotel's plush robes and headed back into the bedroom to discover that Joe had picked up the clothes she'd discarded the night before. He'd also unpacked the rest of her things. They hung beside his at evenly spaced intervals in a wardrobe of ornately carved burled walnut.

"Well," she murmured to her reflection in the wardrobe's mirrored doors, "whatever else the man's done in his checkered past, he learned to pick up after himself."

Evidently you could take the man out of the military. Much harder to take the military out of the man, she mused as she surveyed the sitting room that he'd left in the same neat order. Newspaper folded. Glossy magazines aligned on the monster coffee table. Room service tray with its contents stacked, placed on a hall table near the door. Note folded and propped against the vase centered on a round table inlaid with a dozen different kinds of wood.

The message in the note, like the man himself, was short and succinct.

Checking out film festival venues with Sig. Audi.
Back by 3:00 p.m.

A glance at the mantel clock above a fireplace faced with green marble indicated it was almost 10:00 a.m.

She'd been out cold for thirteen hours. The basic need for sleep taken care of, she now had to deal with another. She'd left Audi Farms last night convinced she'd never eat again. Her stomach was now singing an entirely different tune.

She'd call room service, she decided, and grab a quick shower while waiting for breakfast to be delivered. After that she'd go explore. But first...

She searched the brocade curtains covering the entire wall, hunting for their pull cord then realized they operated electrically. She hit one switch, and the heavy brocade whirred back. A second switch opened the blackout curtain underneath. As soon as it parted, brilliant sunlight flooded in. Momentarily blinded, Callie took a step back and squinted through the glare.

"Oh. My. Lord!"

Stunned, she fumbled for the latch of the double doors that opened onto a wide balcony. A brisk breeze tugged at her hair. The balcony's marble tiles were cold against her bare feet. On the street below, traffic honked and diesel fumes tainted the air. What sounded like a jackhammer was going at it somewhere not too far away. Callie didn't see or hear or feel any of it. The view from the balcony utterly and completely enthralled her.

Naples in all its chaotic glory spilled down the hill below and spread its wide, sprawling arms to embrace the impossibly, incredibly blue Bay of Naples. Vesuvius towered above the far side of the bay. The clouds that had shrouded its peak yesterday had dissipated. Today the cone wore a wreath of glistening white snow.

Enchanted, Callie leaned her elbows on the stone baluster and reveled in her bird's-eye view of jumbled streets and narrow alleys strung with washing and ropes of colored Christmas paper. Far below was what she guessed was the main piazza. A majestic cathedral dominated one side of the square. To its left was a 1890s-looking building with a fanciful glass dome. And facing the cathedral was a mile-long structure with a facade interspersed with dozens of statue-filled niches.

Whirling, Callie rushed back inside. The heck with breakfast. She'd grab a croissant or a roll and some coffee on the go. She had to get out and explore.

She scrambled into slacks and a lightweight sweater, bunched her hair into a scrunchie, slapped on some lip gloss and added a quick postscript to Joe's note. Then she was out the door.

Chapter Six

Callie was almost through the lobby before she remembered Arianna mentioning a street she shouldn't miss. A quick detour took her to the concierge's desk.

"But yes, madam," he said when she asked about a street where they sold crèches. "It is the Via San Gregorio Armeno. Let me show you where it is."

He pulled out a tourist map and circled what looked like a short alleyway but warned her it was difficult to find.

"It's best to take a taxi, madam. And may I suggest other sites nearby worthy of a visit?"

"Yes, please."

"Here, just a few blocks away, is the Museo Cappella Sansevero, with its magnificent statue of the Veiled Christ. And here is the Basilica of San Lorenzo Maggiore. It's located at the exact center of the ancient city of Neapolis. There is a new museum here that gives the history of this area, from the Greeks to the Angevins and down to the present day. You can also visit the excavation of the Roman market once located on this spot."

"Thank you, I will."

"But be careful, madam. These spots are very popular with tourists, and thus with pickpockets. I suggest you drape the strap of your purse across your chest and keep it in front of you, yes?"

Callie thanked him again and studied the map while the bellman summoned a cab. Not that her studying did much good. She gave up even trying to read street signs as the cab rocked through a series of hairpin turns and zoomed down the hill. With each turn the streets got narrower, while the buildings got older, darker and a little grimier.

The taxi driver let her off at the head of the street of the crèche makers. As the concierge had warned, the narrow lane was jammed with tourists. Callie kept a careful hand on the purse she'd looped across her chest and plunged into the throng.

Via San Gregorio Armeno was everything Arianna had said it would be! In shop after shop, brightly lit windows displayed crèches made of wood or cork or gorgeously decoupaged cardboard. Some were small, some huge and multitiered. A number of them featured mechanical windmills or waterfalls or baaing sheep. Artisans were hard at work in many of the shops, hand-painting terra cotta shepherds and oxen and angels.

Other artisans crafted the figures from different eras that fascinated Callie as much as they did the other tourists. Arianna hadn't exaggerated. Statuettes of famous political figures, rock stars and athletes crowded next to the holy family, the magi and the shepherds. Callie recognized a good number. William and Kate with their own little angels. The US president. The Irish musician and world-renowned philanthropist Bono.

As one shopkeeper explained in excellent English, it was the ultimate goal of all Italian entertainers to find themselves on the Via San Gregorio Armeno.

"As soon as they become famous, they want the statue. Here is the great Pavarotti. And the young Anna Tatangelo, who sings like an angel. And this is Giuseppe Fabiano, the footballer who goes to jail for not paying taxes."

Callie dutifully admired the array of modern figures but decided to go traditional on a gift for Joe. The beautifully crafted four-inch statue of Joseph, Mary's husband and protector, depicted both strength and nobility of character. A fitting start to the crèche—and family—she and her very own Joseph might build together.

In another shop she found a Kristoff, the iceman from Disney's *Frozen*, for Tommy, and a flame-haired angel for Dawn. For Kate she chose a wicked caricature of a former US presidential candidate her friend had heartily despised. She left the street pleased with her purchases but not quite sure she fully appreciated the irreverent sense of humor that would juxtapose the sacred and profane so exuberantly.

The tantalizing scent of something hot and yeasty lured her to a bakery halfway down the next block. Since it was already past noon, the cases displayed both pastries and open-faced sandwiches. A slab of pizza bread tempted her, but she decided she'd rather share a real Neapolitan pizza with Joe and settled instead for coffee and a ricotta-filled pastry. Flaky and topped with powdered sugar, the roll melted in her mouth. She lingered over the coffee, people watching and enjoying the hustle of the busy street. She would've stayed longer if not for the desire to be back at the hotel when Joe returned.

Once out on the street, she headed for her next stop. After several wrong turns and an appeal to a passerby for assistance, she found the entrance to Cappella San-severo tucked off a side street. The printed brochure that came with the entrance fee explained that it had once been the private burial chapel of the prince of Sansevero, who'd hired some of Italy's most famous artists and sculptors to embellish his family tomb. The statues and frescoes and painted ceiling were magnificent, but the life-size statue of Christ draped in a thin shroud transfixed Callie. The veil was carved from the same marble block as the statue and was so seemingly transparent that the wounds on Christ's hands, feet and side showed plainly.

She stood by the velvet cord roping off the statue for long moments, only half hearing the Gregorian chant piped into the chapel through hidden speakers. When she finally turned to leave, she was sorry Joe hadn't been there to share the experience with her. So she was both surprised and delighted when a cab pulled up less than a half block later and a tall, broad-shouldered figure emerged.

"Joe! How did you find me?"

"The concierge said…"

The rumble of a truck drowned him out. He waited for it to pass before crossing the narrow street. He was in a suit today. Probably because he'd been meeting with the directors of the Naples film festival and touring the various venues. But he'd tugged off his tie, popped the top buttons on his dress shirt and hooked on a pair of mirrored sunglasses. Callie had to admit he looked as hot in his big-important-executive uniform as he did in his jeans and bomber jacket.

When he'd crossed the narrow street, she greeted him with an eager question. "Have you seen the Sansevero Chapel? It's just down the block."

He hadn't, so Callie made a return visit. The Veiled Christ struck an even deeper chord on second viewing. Its vivid portrayal of Christ's suffering was deeply embedded in her memory when they reemerged into the sunlight filtering through the narrow alley.

"Did you have lunch?" Joe asked.

"Coffee and a roll about an hour ago. I was hoping we could share one of Naples's famous pizzas."

"So was I. Matter of fact, I asked Marcello Audi for the address of his favorite pizza joint. Let's grab a taxi."

His earsplitting whistle brought a cab whipping over to the curb. When he checked an electronic note on his phone and rattled off the address, Callie marveled again at his fluent Italian. She passed the short ride telling him about the mob on the street of the crèche makers and the incredible diversity of nativity figures offered for sale. Only after they'd been shown to a table on the second floor of a tiny restaurant overlooking the bay and placed their order did Callie remark again on the concierge's efficiency in putting Joe on her trail.

"He just told me where you were headed," he said with a shrug. "I tracked you via your phone."

"How?"

"It has a GPS chip."

"Yes, but I thought…"

Confused, she sat back as their aproned waiter delivered their caprese salads and a carafe of chianti. She poked at the thick wedge of mozzarella in the salad, wondering if it came from the Audi farm, while the server poured the ruby-red vino into thick water glasses.

"You thought what?" Joe prompted when the waiter departed.

"I've used the Find My Phone app before to pinpoint its location when I thought I'd lost it. But I thought…no, I'm sure I had to enter my password to access the app."

"You do. I don't."

"Why not?"

"My tech folks developed a program that unscrambles the password."

He said it so calmly, so casually. As if hacking into someone's cell phone was just a routine part of his everyday routine.

"Doesn't the phone have to be turned on to be unscrambled?"

"No."

"So you can track anyone, just by the number?"

"Pretty much." A brief smile flitted across his face. "We offered the program to Homeland Security some weeks back. They want it but are still wrestling with the legalities."

Frowning, Callie poked at her salad again. Although she considered herself a liberal in most respects, the Boston Marathon bombing had tilted her to the right when it came to curtailing the civil liberties of suspected terrorists. She hardly fell into that category, however.

Still frowning, she met Joe's bland gaze. "I'm not sure I like the idea of being on an electronic leash."

"Comes with the ring, sweetheart."

The blunt, masculine possessiveness behind that statement left her sputtering indignantly.

"Dammit, Joe. The fact that I'm wearing your ring doesn't mean I want you to take control of my life."

A shuttered look dropped over his face, spurring her irritation.

"I appreciate your wanting to look out for me," she said firmly. "I do *not*, however, appreciate you preempting my decisions. Like letting Carlo know I'd decided to accept his offer before I had a chance to tell him myself. Or arranging this weekend in Naples, as delightful as it is, when I have so much to do in Rome. Or..."

"I protect what's mine." His eyes had gone cold. "Any way I have to."

A hot retort rose to Callie's lips. She bit it back as she remembered the little bit of his past that he'd shared with her on the drive down from Rome.

"The woman you smuggled out of Angola. The one killed by an assassin in Curaçao. Were you...were you in love with her?"

A muscle ticked in one side of his jaw. He sat unmoving, his expression so closed she thought he wouldn't answer. When he did, she had to strain to hear him.

"I'm not sure you'd call it love. Nattat was fiery and outspoken. And so damned uncompromising. We argued as often as we..."

He broke off, leaving Callie to fill in the blanks. Right. They'd argued as often as they'd indulged in wild, animal sex.

She dropped suddenly clenched fists to her lap. She'd never for one moment imagined she could be jealous of a dead woman.

"She wore her tribal headdress like a badge of honor," Joe continued after a moment. "She hated the Portuguese who'd plundered her country. Hated the native-born Angolans doing the same. As the youngest member ever elected to parliament, she was an unrelenting thorn in their sides." His jaw worked. "It was only a matter of time until the bastards got to her."

The jealousy bit harder, sharper. Callie couldn't imagine a greater contrast between herself and a young, passionate Angolan member of parliament. She suspected Joe had never categorized this crusader for human rights as a calm port to come home to.

Ashamed of the thought and green-eyed monster nipping at her, Callie said quietly, "She sounds like an amazing woman, Joe."

"Yeah. Amazing. Also stubborn as hell and too prone to take risks."

"Which I'm not."

He hiked a brow.

"Okay, I may be a little stubborn at times," she conceded, "but I'm not inclined to take risks. So I don't need to be wrapped in cotton wool. Or kept on an electronic leash."

He didn't like it. She could tell by his closed expression.

"I mean it, Joe. We have to respect each other's boundaries."

He gave that a polite few moments' consideration before shaking his head. "I'm not made that way, Callie. I can't turn it on and off."

She stared across the table with a confusing sense of having reached an impasse. Intellectually, she flatly rejected the idea of being considered any man's possession. Training and experience, however, had taught her some primitive instincts were so deeply imprinted on homo sapiens' DNA that society's civilizing influences could never eradicated. The instinct to protect one's mate was certainly one of those instincts.

Unfortunately, she'd worked too many cases where that protective, possessive instinct spilled into jealousy and domestic violence. Could that happen with Joe? Given his admittedly violent past and dangerous present occupation, Callie couldn't deny the possibility. Yet every primitive instinct *she* possessed said she had nothing to fear from him.

Still, they needed to establish some of those boundaries she'd mentioned now, before they went too far down the path to misunderstanding or distrust. Their pizza arrived before she could marshal her arguments, however. Just as well, she decided. Better to finish this discussion back at the hotel, in the privacy of their opulent suite.

"Ecco! Pizza margherita."

The waiter positioned the pie on the stand in the center of the table with a dramatic flourish and proceeded to serve them a piece. The single slice slopped over the edge of Callie's plate and smelled of crusty dough, sweet tomatoes, mozzarella and fresh basil. Her first bite confirmed it tasted even better than it looked.

"Oh, God! This is unreal." She took another bite, swiping at strings of cheese and savoring the explosion of spices and sauce. "Do you know why they call it *pizza margherita*?" she asked Joe. "I read somewhere it's named after a queen."

"Right. The wife of King Umberto the first or second. Maybe third." He caught a wayward mozzarella strand, tucked it back on his half-devoured slice. "When Umberto and his wife visited Naples and tried pizza for the first time, she said the colors reminded her of the Italian flag."

Callie could see why. The bright red tomatoes. The white mozzarella. The green of the basil leaves.

"So they named it after her," she commented. "Would

those be the same royals who built that humongous palace in the main piazza?"

"Their descendants, I'd guess, a couple centuries removed." He downed another man-sized bite. "The palace is on the way back to the hotel. It's pretty impressive. We could tour it, if you'd like."

"I would. And tomorrow, we *have* to visit Pompeii before we head up to Rome."

"Deal."

They opted for a self-guided tour of the grand palace, aided by a free app they downloaded to their cell phones. The wide marble staircase was impressive enough. The opulence of the salons above boggled Callie's mind. The salons ran into each other, one after another. The blue room. The red. The gold. Each containing priceless works of art, lavishly decorated baroque furniture and some really strange objects brought from the four corners of the world as gifts for the Bourbon kings. Joe held the sack with her purchases while Callie spun in slow circles, her phone to her ear, trying to take in the magnificence.

Pleasantly tired after her day of exploring, she relaxed against Joe's side during the taxi ride back to the hotel. She'd enjoyed the afternoon so much that she toyed with the idea of just taking things with Joe as they came, one speed bump at a time. Especially since those little bumps occurred between stretches of such thrilling and intense pleasure.

Like the stretch that began after they crossed the lobby and the elevator doors pinged shut. In a swift move, Joe backed her against the paneled wall. His mouth came down on hers, hard and hungry and demanding the response that flared instantly in her belly.

She didn't even try to temper it. Didn't hold back. *Couldn't* hold back. There was nothing gentle in the kiss. Nothing tame or affectionate. The heat in it ignited an answering flame that she knew burned hot in her face when he raised his head.

"Been waiting to do this since I picked you up at the airport yesterday morning. Damned near killed me when jet lag got to you last night." He dipped his head, took another taste, muttered against her lips, "Tell me the palace didn't wipe you out."

Since his hands were as busy as his mouth, Callie could only gasp an urgent negative. "The palace… didn't…wipe me…out."

The hum that rose from his throat conveyed equal parts relief, satisfaction and a hunger so fierce that every nerve in her body leaped with anticipation. She had time for only a fleeting prayer that the elevator wouldn't stop to let anyone else on before it hit their floor. Then Joe raked both hands into her hair, dislodging the scrunchie, and wedged a knee between hers. His mouth devouring hers once more, he rocked her with a pleasure so intense she almost lost it right there.

The elevator made it to their floor without any stops, thank God, and their suite was only a few doors down the hall. Callie spent those few yards raking a hand through the hair now tumbling around her face and tugging at the hem of her sweater. A useless exercise, since Joe swept her into his arms as soon as he'd keyed the door. Her sweater rucked up again and her hair got caught against his shoulder, but she didn't even wince when the kick he aimed at the door sent it banging into the jamb.

He had to dip to set the security lock and flip on the electronic Do Not Disturb sign. Callie grabbed his shoulders to keep from being upended and held on as he cut through the sitting room. She was still clinging like a monkey when they hit the bedroom.

Housekeeping had been in, she saw as Joe made straight for the four-poster draped in champagne-colored silk. The gold tassels decorating the bed's richly embroidered comforter marched in a straight line along its hem. A half dozen or more similarly tasseled pillows in varying shapes and sizes sat banked against the carved headboard.

They promptly shot all that neat precision to hell. Joe didn't take time to yank down the spread. Didn't bother shoving the pillows out of the way. He dropped to the bed with Callie still locked against him.

She wasn't sure who attacked whose clothes first. They probably went at it simultaneously. She got his dress shirt off without too much trouble, but Joe was quieter and much quicker. He was feasting on her bare breast while she was still trying to shove his slacks down his lean, muscular flanks. Frustrated, she nipped him on the shoulder. Then nipped again, harder.

That got his attention. His head shot up. Surprise glinted in his eyes.

"You trying to tell me something, tiger?"

"Yes," she panted.

The surprise deepened. "Interesting. Didn't think you were into rough stuff."

"I'm not!" She wiggled under him, fighting the slacks again. "But I could use a little help here."

When he rolled to one side and shucked the rest of his clothes, Callie didn't hesitate. Taking full advantage of having him on his back, she swung a leg over his hip even before his shoes and pants hit the floor. A quick push brought her upright. Another wiggle scooted her back a few inches. Straddling his thighs, she had full access to his rampant sex.

He was rock hard and slick to her touch. And salty when she scooted back a few more inches and contorted enough to take him in her mouth. She couldn't remember ever doing this before. Couldn't remember wanting to. Yet having Joe at the mercy of *her* hands and thighs and busy, busy lips shot her into a new sexual stratosphere. She'd gone beyond registering anything other than his taste and his scent and his feel when he gave a hoarse grunt that could have signaled pleasure or protest.

"Callie. Sweetheart." He nudged her shoulders. "Let me... Crap!"

Joe being Joe, he insisted on giving her the same pleasure she'd given him. Much to Callie's secret delight, however, it took him a few moments to recoup his strength. Hiding a grin, she wallowed in a trough of feminine superiority right up until the moment he had her digging her nails into the spread and moaning in a long, shuddering, shattering release.

It was a while before they recovered enough to sluice off in the mammoth shower and wrap up from neck to knees in the hotel's plush terry-cloth robes. As Callie walked back into the bedroom busily towel drying her hair, Joe winced at the red scrape on her neck.

"Sorry 'bout that whisker burn."

She looked up from under the towel and smiled. "No complaints on this side. It was worth... Oh!"

She stopped dead. Eyes round, jaw slack, she gaped at the scene outside their floor-to-ceiling windows. Dusk had begun to darken the sky, and a fat, full moon hung just above the stone balustrade of their balcony.

"It's just like in that song," she breathed in delight. "The one about the moon hitting your eye like a big pizza pie."

Whipping back her hair, she wrapped the towel turban-style around the still-damp mass and shoved her feet into the hotel-provided slippers.

"Let's go out on the veranda."

"Go ahead. I'll get some Pellegrino and join you."

While she arrowed straight for the veranda, Joe detoured to the minibar to retrieve two dew-streaked bottles. The chilled water in hand, he took a moment to study the robed and turbaned figure transfixed by her view of the moon-washed bay. She'd turned up the collar on the robe and belted it tighter around her waist against the cooling evening air. Elbows propped on the railing, she leaned forward just far enough to showcase her nice, trim butt.

God, she was gorgeous. She didn't think so. No surprise there. She'd grown up in the shadow of her two friends and tended to retreat into the background whenever Kate or Dawn took center stage. Not because they were smarter or prettier or more accomplished. Because she was so comfortable in her own skin that she felt no need to compete for attention. Which was one of the reasons Joe had known almost immediately Callie Langston was right for him. He admired her quiet presence. Envied her serenity.

He didn't have much of either in his own life. Not that he lived on a razor's edge 24/7. Sometimes he went months between a high-profile client like Carlo di Lorenzo or a seriously vulnerable target like the Naples film festival. Even on the job, Joe had learned to make stress work for him. It kept him and his team alert. Kept them alive. It was those few hours when the adrenaline rocketed through the roof, those days and nights when sleep wasn't an option, that left him craving a quiet sanctuary to return to after a particularly hairy gig.

He did have a sanctuary or two already. He maintained a house close to his operations base in Houston. Kept a private retreat in the Colorado Rockies. Paid a month-to-month lease on apartment in LA used for strictly business purposes. The places were comfortable. Some might say luxurious. But sterile. Empty. He wanted someone like Callie to fill that emptiness.

Joe's fists tightened on the bottles. No, dammit! He didn't want someone *like* Callie. He wanted *her*.

Looking back, he knew now that he hadn't wanted Nattat this badly. Yeah, he'd lusted for her. Broken every rule in the book for her. Even killed for her. But she'd never stirred this gut-deep need to cherish and protect and…and…

Hell! No point trying to analyze whatever it was Callie stirred in him. Enough to just roll with it. Which he did, at least until she straightened and came inside.

"It's colder than it looks out there," she announced with a little shiver.

He hefted the Pellegrino. "Want something that'll raise more heat than water?"

"No, that's good. Besides, after all that wine we had with our pizza, I need to have a clear head."

"For?"

She gave the ends of the robe's belt a little tug. "I enjoyed today, Joe. This whole weekend. But we need to talk."

Chapter Seven

We need to talk.

Exactly what every man wanted to hear from his woman. Hiding a grimace, Joe arched a brow. "Long talk or short?"

"That depends on you."

His euphoric mood of just a few seconds ago went down in flames. Just your basic crash and burn, he thought sardonically as he gestured to the sitting room.

"Might as well get comfortable."

She curled into one end of the curved-back sofa and tucked her feet under her. Joe took the middle cushion. Not close enough to crowd her, but within reaching distance. Just in case he had to resort to emergency measures. Passing her one of the bottles, he braced for the worst while she unscrewed the cap and took a long swallow.

"I debated whether to have this discussion, Joe. I enjoyed this afternoon so much. This whole weekend. Especially the past few hours," she added with smile.

The smile didn't hack it. "Cut to the chase, Callie. What's this about?"

Unperturbed by the gruff demand, she nodded. "All right. You told me you're not into flowery phrases or stringing together lots of adjectives, so let's keep it simple. If you had to describe what you feel for me in just two or three words, what would they be? And *please* don't say 'a calm port in a storm.'"

Christ! Where'd that come from? He'd thought… been sure…she'd understood it was a compliment. Digging deep, he settled on some lines of Scripture his gran had drilled into him as a kid, accompanied more often than not by the smack of her palm alongside his head.

"Three words? How about 'faith, hope and love. But,'" he added gruffly, "'the greatest of these is love.'"

Her eyes widened in surprise. *Payback*, he thought with a stab of fierce satisfaction, *for the crash and burn.*

"Isn't that from the Bible?"

"First Corinthians, chapter thirteen."

"I didn't know… That is…" She floundered for another moment. "Are you a regular churchgoer?"

"Not according to my grandmother."

"You have a grandmother?" she echoed faintly.

"Most people do," he drawled.

"You've never mentioned her. Or your parents. Are they still alive?"

"Never knew my father. Mom died when I was six. Gran took over then."

"Is she still alive?"

"Alive and kicking. She lives only a few blocks from me in Houston."

It'd taken some persuasion to get the feisty octogenarian to leave the home she'd raised him in. Joe had made sure she was comfortable there, that house had every modern convenience known to man. But three years ago arthritis all but crippled her and Joe finally convinced her to move to Houston. She was in a wheelchair now and quoting Bible scriptures to the attendants at a luxurious assisted-living center.

"How often do you…?" She stopped, drew a breath. "Never mind. We'll get to that later."

He waited, letting her circle back to whatever had spurred this need for this little talk.

"Why 'faith, hope and love'?" she finally questioned.

Resigned, Joe dug a little deeper. "Faith, because once you give your loyalty, it stays given. Dawn and Kate are living proof of that."

"I guess," she murmured, not quite convinced.

"Hope, because…" He held that deep purple gaze. "For the first time in longer than I can remember, the future holds promise."

Her doubt melted, her voice softened. "And love? Are you in love with me, Joe?"

What the hell? Did she think he went around proposing to every female who looked at him sideways?

"You're the first…the only…woman I've asked to marry me."

"So that's a yes?"

"Didn't I just say that?"

"Not exactly. Say the words. I'd like to hear them."

He opened his mouth, but her too-innocent expression knocked the simple phrase back down his throat. The little witch! She was jacking him. Playing him like a trout on the end of a six-pound line.

"I love you. And now…" Thunking his Pellegrino down on the coffee table, he plucked hers out of her hand and leaned in. "Your turn. What do you feel for me? Three words. Spit 'em out."

She didn't blink, didn't hesitate. "I love you. I didn't realize how much until this moment."

"Right. Okay. Good."

Callie knew better than to smile, but it took some doing. He sounded every bit as flustered as she had a few moments ago. Taking pity on his obvious confusion, she laid a hand on his forearm.

"Will it help if I tell you that you're the first man... the *only* man...whose ring I've worn?"

"It helps," he said, recovering. "It also makes me wonder where this 'we need to talk' sh...stuff came from."

She acknowledged the barb with a nod and took a moment to gather her thoughts. Her religious education had been sporadic at best. One parent was a lapsed Catholic, the other agnostic. They'd both pretty much left her to find her own way. But she'd attended enough weddings to have more than a passing familiarity with the love verse Joe had just quoted.

"Isn't there something in that First Corinthians chapter about love not insisting on having its own way?"

"Verse five. Why? What's your point?"

"Remember what you said this afternoon? When I told you I don't like being on an electronic leash?"

"Hell, Callie. Is that what this is all about? The phone-tracking app?"

"The app's part of it. Mostly it's about establishing and respecting the boundaries I mentioned."

She chewed on the inside of her cheek, needing to get this right. Whatever future they might build together depended on the next few moments.

"You told me you couldn't turn your instincts off and on, Joe. I don't want you to turn them off. Not completely. Some primitive corner of my psyche thrills to the idea of a strong, protective mate."

He managed to look both vindicated and baffled. "I repeat, what's your point?"

"The point," she said patiently, "is that I want to be a full partner in this relationship, not some pampered pet. I want you to explain up front about any security issues or actions that involve me. Or us. Or you, for that matter."

"The process isn't always that deliberate. There are times…too many times…when I have to go with my gut."

"I get that. I do. And I'd be a fool to tell you to ignore those gut instincts. It's the other times. The ordinary you-and-me times. I need to know you won't just assume you know best for me."

She reached for his hand. Hers was still damp and chilled from the Pellegrino bottle, his warm and sinewy. The contrast wasn't lost on her.

They were so different, she and Joe. They came from disparate backgrounds, apparently. Had followed widely divergent career paths. And they were certainly at the opposite ends of the spectrum when it came to bruising, bare-knuckle experiences.

And yet in many ways they were very much alike. Both self-contained. Both confident of their own abilities. Both, she thought with a warm halo around her heart, seemingly in this for the long haul.

"Promise you won't make unilateral decisions, except in extraordinary circumstances."

He grabbed at the out. "Extraordinary circumstances. Okay, I can live with that."

"I mean it, Joe. Starting here, starting now, we're equal partners in this adventure. Deal?"

He thought about it for a second or two, then raised her hand and dropped a kiss on the back of it. The gesture was so courtly and un-Joe-like that she almost melted into a puddle right there on the hotel's thousand-dollar-plus sofa.

"Deal."

He released her fingers and reached for the belt of her robe instead. It loosened with a single tug. With a satisfied grunt, he curved his palm over her thigh.

"As your full and equal partner, I vote we adjourn to the bed."

"The bed we just left a few moments ago?"

"Yeah." He slid his hand higher. "That one."

A cold, gray drizzle obscured the bay the next morning, but Callie held Joe to his promise to take her to Pompeii before they drove up to Rome. Fortified by the hotel's sumptuous Sunday brunch, they checked out and hit the road.

The nasty weather actually did them a favor by whittling the hordes of tourists down to the hardiest few. Bundled against the chill in her long duster and the paisley scarf looped twice around her neck, European-style, Callie shoved her left hand in her pocket. Joe held onto her right and kept it tucked in the pocket of his leather jacket.

She appreciated his steadying grip as they navigated the cobbled streets. Drifting fingers of fog made the time-worn stones slick and treacherous. They also blanketed the ancient ruin in eerie silence, almost as if the terror of that day in 79 AD had never happened. Yet every excavated dwelling, every scrap of tiled floor or line of decapitated marble columns rising out of the mist gave grim evidence of Vesuvius's destructive power.

"Hard to believe all this lay buried for more than a thousand years," she murmured.

Even harder to believe the hot ash and molten lava had spewed out of the volcano with such speed that Pompeii's citizens had no time or place to run. They had died where they cowered. Or in the case of a noticeably pregnant woman, where she lay. Callie bit her lip as she studied the plaster cast made from the hardened hollow where the woman's body had once been entombed in layers of ash. She'd tried to shield her head with one arm. The other cradled her stomach and unborn babe.

The tragic figure had Callie blinking back tears. She couldn't help thinking of Kate and her emerging baby bump. She hated to miss her friend's exciting time of discovery and impending birth. Hated missing Christmas with Dawn and her new family, too. Her choice, she reminded herself. Her choice. But she made a silent promise to call her friends as soon as she got settled in her new apartment.

That led to a reminder of the job waiting in Rome and the center sheltering desperate female refugees. She stared at the cast of the long-dead woman, thinking that all these years later, death and destruction still rained down from the skies. Man-made now, more often than not, and every bit as devastating. So many tried to escape it. So many needed help.

"I've seen enough," she told Joe. "Let's go."

The dank, heavy mist continued to roll in from the coast as they drove north. Traffic moved at a slow crawl for most of the way. When they finally crested one of Rome's seven fabled hills, angry black clouds had piled up over the city and added to the fast-descending darkness.

The deluge hit moments later. As if navigating the capital's labyrinthine center wasn't enough of a challenge, the torrential downpour turned to slush, then fat, wet snowflakes that gave the SUV's oversize wipers a run for their money. With grim thanks for GPS, Joe followed the system's precise directions to the flat he'd checked out before picking Callie up at the airport three days ago. The parking gods must have been smiling. He squeezed into a space just a few yards from the entrance, unloaded their carryalls and caught Callie's arm for a quick dash through the snow.

The flat wasn't much. One bedroom, one combination kitchen, eating area and living room, with a tiny bath tucked in a corner. But it was on the third floor of a recently renovated building with solid security and located only a few blocks from the women's center where she'd be working. Still, he'd had Emilio, his contact here in Rome, install a fingerprint-activated electronic keypad on her door and new bolts on the windows…which, under the terms of their recently negotiated agreement, he felt obligated to tell her about.

"Was that really necessary?" she asked, eyeing the polished brass hardware that gleamed bright and new against an old but very solid door.

"Probably not. Here, press your palm against the scanner. Fingers flat. Now roll them a little. Right to left. Good."

Feeling a little like a felon being fingerprinted by Rome's *polizia*, she submitted to what she hoped was the last of Joe's electronic gadgets.

"The super has an override code," he said as the door clicked open. "Just in case."

Callie didn't move. "Do you have the code, too?"

"Yeah, I do." He turned and gave her a cool look. "You have a problem with that?"

"Not if you call or text me before you use it."

"Damn." His mouth twisted. "There goes my plan to surprise you when you come home and find me wearing nothing but a smile and big red bow."

It was so deadpan—and so unexpected—that Callie blinked before choking out a laugh. "Trust me. If I walk in and find you in a big red bow, I'll be *extremely* surprised."

"Too late. You ruined it. I'll think up something else." He nudged the door with his carryall. "You want in or not?"

Once inside, Joe flicked on the lights and waited while Callie explored her new home.

It was perfect, she thought in delight. Absolutely perfect. The warm yellow walls dispelled the winter gloom, and the furnishings were an eclectic mix of modern and shabby chic. The kitchen consisted of a two-burner stove with a single-rack oven, a small fridge and cloth-covered cupboards. The eating area held only a narrow drop-leaf table and two chairs that could be turned around to augment seating in the living area. That room's solitary window faced the street and the buildings directly opposite. Roll-down shutters would block the streetlights and traffic noise.

Entranced, she opened a door to the bathroom. A stool, a sink and a shower surrounded by a circular curtain suspended from the ceiling, all squeezed into what she guessed might once have been a closet.

The bedroom just beyond contained only a double bed, a nightstand and a hand-painted wardrobe. But to Callie's great joy, it also boasted a glass-paned door that opened onto a minuscule balcony that seemed to hang suspended in midair. Snow-dusted buildings stair-stepped down the steep hill below. And in the distance a floodlit dome was just visible through the curtain of snow.

"Is that St. Peter's?" she gasped.

"Looks like."

Thrilled, she twisted the knob and stepped outside for a better look. Skirting a dime-size café table with a single chair, she gripped the wrought-iron railing with gloved hands. Rome had enchanted her during her brief visit with Dawn and Kate a few months ago. Awestruck by the snowy scene spread out before her, she fell completely, irrevocably in love.

More in love, she amended as Joe edged past the rickety little table to join her. Overwhelmed, she turned and framed his face with her gloved hands. The light spilling through the glass-paned door illuminated one side of his face. The scar was lost in shadow. Where it belonged, she thought fiercely. His past had made him the man he was now, but the future belonged to her. To both of them.

"Thank you," she breathed. "For Naples. For Pompeii. For being here with me. This whole day's been perfect."

"You're welcome. It'll be even more perfect," he added with a hopeful waggle of his brows, "if Emilio stocked your kitchen with something quick and easy to fix."

From the sublime to the practical. Laughing, Callie came back to earth.

And now that he'd mentioned it, she was ravenous, too. After that ginormous brunch at the hotel in Naples, she'd vowed to cut out all carbs for the next week. Touring Pompeii and the long, slow drive back to Rome sent that vow down the tubes.

"Let's take a look."

They shed their coats and crowded into the tiny kitchen. Emilio had indeed stocked the fridge and tiny pantry. Callie inventoried paper-wrapped Parma ham, a thick wedge of Asiago cheese, garlic cloves, onions, Roma tomatoes, potatoes, eggs, coffee, creamer, some canned soup, a bottle of Tuscan red and, of course, several variations of pasta.

"How about an omelet?" she suggested. "That's quick and easy."

"I hit the omelet bar at breakfast."

"Soup?"

"Tell you what. I spotted a trattoria on the corner. Why don't I just go down and get two takeout orders of veal scaloppine?"

"Oh, God, that sounds wonderful. But I hate for you to go back out in the snow."

"Not a problem." He snagged his jacket off the chair where he'd draped it. "I'll be right back. You open the wine and get settled."

Before she accomplished either of those tasks, Callie had a far more important one to attend to. It was just past six Rome time. A little after noon in DC. Digging her phone out of her purse, she dropped onto the edge of the bed and hit Kate's speed-dial number.

"Callie! Travis and I were just talking about you. How's Rome?"

"Absolutely incredible." Her gaze locked on the window. "At this precise moment I'm sitting on the side of the bed in my apartment, looking through the balcony door, watching snow blanket the dome of St. Peter's."

"Get. Out."

"I kid you not! Hold on while I get Dawn on the line."

Their friend answered on the second ring and shouted over the din in the background. "About time you called."

"What?"

"I said, it's about time you called."

"I can barely hear you. Where are you?"

"Sunday brunch at Paoli's. Where are *you*, and more important, what the heck took you so long to contact your best friends?"

"I've been a little busy."

"That's what I tried to tell her," Kate put in. "She wanted to call you, but I twisted her arm and made her wait until you got your feet on the ground."

"I waited," Dawn groused, "but I didn't like it. So spill it, girl. No! Hold on, I need to go someplace without all these decibels."

Callie heard a thump, a muffled voice, the clash of pots and pans. Then blessed silence.

"Okay," Dawn announced breathlessly. "I'm in the ladies' room. Wait a sec while I put the seat down. There. I'm good. Now talk. How's Rome? What's happening with you and Joe?"

"Rome is clean and bright and dusted with snow from top to bottom. And Joe…"

Callie didn't spin out the pause deliberately. She just needed a couple seconds to sort through everything that had happened in the three tumultuous days since she'd landed in Italy.

"We've been together this whole time. After he picked me up at the airport Friday morning, we drove down to Naples to meet with his prospective client. Then…"

"Wait. Back up. You crawl off a plane after a nine-hour flight and he takes you to Naples for a business meeting?"

"Actually, we went for a sort of pre-Christmas feast with Signor Audi and his family. At their water buffalo ranch."

Dawn made a "huh" noise but Kate caught the connection immediately.

"Buffalo, as in mozzarella cheese?"

"As in a dozen different varieties of mozzarella, all of them scrumptious."

"And you went to the source of these dozen different varieties?"

"We did! Honestly, it was so interesting. The buffalo get scrubbed, massaged, milked and scrubbed again. All done robotically."

"Sounds fascinating," Dawn commented in a voice that clearly indicated otherwise. "Back to Joe. Three whole days with Mr. If I Tell You I'll Have to Kill You, and you haven't changed your mind?"

"No," Callie said at the same moment the sound of a loud flush came through the phone. "Just the opposite."

"What? I can't hear you."

"I said Joe and I are great. Fantastic. Wonderful."

"Wow," Dawn murmured after a short silence. "Those must have been some three days."

"They were. I'll zip off an email tomorrow with all the juicy details."

"And pictures," Kate insisted. "We want pictures of your apartment and where you work."

"Will do. Say hi to Travis and Brian and Tommy. I love you all and miss you already."

"Give Joe our best. And Carlo, when you see him."

"Will do," Callie promised again. "Ciao for now."

She clicked off and pushed off the bed. Her first

order of business was to uncork the wine and let it breathe. She wasted a few moments hunting for a cork-screw until she realized the cap was a twist-off. Interesting. One of her coworkers back in Boston had been a self-professed and completely unapologetic wine snob. Devin would no doubt have heart palpitations if he had to twist rather than uncork and meticulously decant.

Smiling at the thought, she went ahead and set the table with the silverware and pretty red-and-yellow napkins she'd found in her hunt for a corkscrew. No wine goblets, but the wavy green water glasses would do nicely.

That homey task done, she transferred the carryalls to the bedroom. She left Joe's on the bed but unpacked her toiletries and stuffed the clothes she'd worn over the weekend in the laundry bag she found hanging in the hand-painted wardrobe. Her two suitcases were in the wardrobe, too, left there by the so-efficient Emilio. She pulled one out, but before she could lug it to the bed to unpack, her phone chirped. The succinct text message made her grin.

Coming up. Using the override.

Ha! Who said you couldn't teach an old dog new tricks? Still grinning, Callie went to join Joe for her first meal in her new home.

Chapter Eight

Joe stayed the night, taking up more than his fair share of the double bed, and had to leave early Monday morning.

"I'll be in Zurich until Wednesday," he told Callie as he tucked his shaving kit into his carryall. "Then I have to fly back to the States. You've got Emilio's number. Call him if you need anything before I get back."

"Any idea when that might be?"

"Not sure. I'll try to make it before Christmas, but I have to put together the team I promised Marcello Audi I'd bring in the first week in January. Some top people to beef up electronic surveillance at his venue sites. More to conduct hands-on training for his security staff."

She nodded but suffered another silent qualm about the prospect of spending Christmas on her own in Italy. Her decision, she reminded herself fiercely as Joe zipped his carryall. Her decision.

Besides, if the center was as short-staffed as Carlo had indicated, she wouldn't have time to feel lonely. Or so she thought, right up until she walked Joe to the door of her tiny apartment.

"Have a safe trip home."

"Plan to." He curled a knuckle under her chin and tipped her face to his. "Good luck at the center. You sure you can find it?"

"Two blocks to the north and one to the east? I think so. But if I have any trouble," she promised solemnly, "I'll use the directional finder on my phone."

"Whatever works." He took the hit with a philosophical shrug and made a slow pass over her lower lip with his thumb. "Don't let the heartache you find there get you too down."

Easier said than done, she knew. She still carried painful memories of some of the children's cases she'd worked in her heart.

"I plan to stay too busy to get down."

"After meeting *il Drago*, I can pretty much guarantee you will."

"*Il Drago?* The dragon? I hope that doesn't refer to my new boss."

"Carlo's tag for her, not mine. It fits, though. The woman put us both through the wringer when he told her I wanted to review the center's refugee screening process."

"Wonderful. You pissed off my new boss. Exactly what I needed to hear before my first day on the job."

His mouth curved in one of his rare grins. "My money's on you, Pansy Eyes. Just aim one of your cool, we-need-to-talk looks at her and she'll fold like *washi*. Thin Japanese paper," he said in answer to her blank look. "They use it make origami and wrap gifts to burn in honor of their ancestors."

This man amazed her. He really did. Bible verses. Japanese origami. Fiery tribal beauties. Hired assassins. She was still trying to fit all these facets of his personality into their respective niches when he dropped a quick kiss on her lips.

"Call me," he ordered as he headed down the narrow S-shaped stairs. "Let me know how today goes."

"I will."

He'd hit the first floor landing before she remembered the Christmas gifts she'd purchased in Naples. She leaned over the railing to call him back, but he was already out the door.

Damn! He could've taken Dawn's and Kate's and Tommy's back to the States with him. Opened his, too, while he was here. She'd have to FedEx the others and keep his until his return to Rome. Hopefully in time for Christmas.

She gave the high-tech palm pad a sideways glance as she wandered back into her new home. Joe's presence had made the two rooms seem cozy. Okay, crowded. Now they felt empty, sucked of their vitality.

All right. Enough of that. She had things to do, places to go, people to see. With a determined roll of her shoulders, Callie shook off her deflated feeling and set to work unpacking the suitcases Emilio had delivered.

Not that she had all that much to unpack. She'd based her wardrobe choices on a study of Rome's average winter temperatures and her preliminary research into the shelter run by International Aid to Displaced Women. The center's residents were older than the children she'd worked with for the past six years. They'd lost their husbands, their families, all ties to their native lands.

Some had survived unimaginable horrors. Callie knew they'd relate more to jeans and a sweater than a tailored black pantsuit.

An hour later she emerged into a city that had come alive after its snowy night. The sun was a bright sphere, the air frosty. Tucking her chin in her scarf and her hands deep in the pockets of her duster, Callie set off for the center.

The Monday morning traffic had churned the streets to slush, but the wrought-iron balconies and green-painted shutters adorning the buildings on both sides of the street still sported downy white eyebrows. School kids with monster book bags clumped by in oversize boots. Housewives bundled up against the cold clutched fishnet shopping bags as they headed to the local butchers and greengrocers. Office workers stood elbow to elbow at espresso bars, munching pastries, scanning folded newspapers and getting the necessary caffeine jolt to jump-start their day.

When a patron exited one of those tiny cafés, the scent of fresh-ground coffee and hot croissants lured Callie inside. She studied the chalkboard menu while waiting in line and managed to order in her few phrases of broken Italian. The white chocolate cream concoction came in a glass with a silver handle and was topped with a frothy heart almost too pretty to slurp. She carried it and a still-warm croissant to a stand-up counter and consumed both while studying the framed black-and-white photos filling every square inch of wall space.

Many were from WWII and depicted US soldiers who must have chosen this little café as a favorite gathering spot. Others looked like they were from the late '40s and early '50s. Callie spotted an extremely well-endowed Sophia Loren in one, a Jack Kennedy look-alike in another.

Intrigued, she edged closer to examine the scrawled signature. It *was* Kennedy. Young, impossibly handsome, flashing that famous grin, with his arm hooked over the back of a chair occupied by a pouty blonde Callie didn't recognize. She would've liked to take a closer look at some of the other celebrities, but a quick glance at the clock above the bar sent her back out into the bright, cold morning.

A quick turn brought her to her new place of employment. Identified only by the street number above its door, the three-story building that housed the IADW center blended in with its neighbors. Like them, it was stuccoed, only this was a deeper terra-cotta red than either of its neighbors. Marble pediments decorated the first-floor windows; green shutters framed the others. Callie noted the absence of any security cameras and felt a tingle at the back of her neck as she remembered Joe's comment about terrorists using refugee centers as conduits to the West.

Although he hadn't mentioned it—probably because he hadn't wanted to scare her—she suspected these centers could become targets, too, for extremists at both ends of the spectrum. Ultra-right neo-Nazi types stirred to fury over the influx of "foreigners" might present as much of a threat as leftist revolutionaries seeking to exploit the residents' hopes and fears.

With these—hopefully remote!—possibilities in mind, she pressed the bell centered in a dented and slightly rusted speaker box.

"Si?"

The single syllable came across as clipped and distinctly impatient.

"My name is Callie Langston. I'm…"

"Finally! Come in. I'm in the storeroom. Down the hall, last door on the right."

The locked clicked, and Callie stepped into a foyer tiled in gray marble. A graceful arch led from the foyer to a long hallway. Doors opened off either side of the hall, and at the far end a graceful marble staircase spiraled upward.

She made her way to the last door on the right as instructed while admiring the Murano glass sconces and elaborate ceiling medallions that suggested the center had once been home to a fairly well-to-do family. She was only a few feet from her destination when a thump and a curse sounded from its open door. A quick glance inside showed a cluttered office and a rail-thin woman with short, flyaway white hair. While Callie watched, the woman shoved aside a carton with a logo that depicted what looked like a giant green hand cupping a dark-eyed baby in its palm.

The hearty shove sent the box careening into a stack of similarly marked cartons. They wobbled wildly, precipitating another muttered curse and a quick jump forward from Callie. Between them, the two women managed to keep the tower more or less upright.

The save didn't appear to afford the older woman much satisfaction. Hands on hips, she scowled at the stack, as if daring it to take another wobble. Only after she'd stared it down did she turn a look of unalloyed disgust on Callie.

"I've told this group again and again we need supplies for women and adolescent girls."

Her English was thick and heavily accented.

"Do they listen? No! Do they keep sending diapers and teething rings? Yes! Does my *idiota* intern accept their shipments? Every time!"

Despite her skeletal thinness and dandelion-fine white hair, she looked so fierce Callie half expected her to aim another kick at the precariously stacked boxes. Instead, she drilled the newcomer with a pair of startlingly blue eyes.

"The prince insisted I take you on as my deputy. Your credentials are impressive, I'll give you that. Far better than the one you're replacing. But if you think working with us at the center will convince the prince to offer more than weekends in Monte Carlo or Antibes, you should think again."

"*Excuse* me?"

"Ah! So he didn't tell you? No, of course he would not. He will wait for the right moment."

"Look, Signora Alberti… You are Signora Alberti, aren't you?"

"*Sì.*"

"Look, Signora Alberti. The prince is a friend. A good friend. But if you don't wish to accept me based on my credentials, that's your prerogative."

"*Magari.*"

"I'm sorry," Callie said stiffly. "I don't know that word."

"It means… How do you say in America? *I wish.*"

Callie opened her mouth, but before she could tell the Wicked Witch of the East to take her job and stuff it, the director flapped an impatient hand.

"*Non importa.* I will know soon enough if you're as hopeless as the others. Come along. I'll introduce you to the staff who aren't in session. You'll meet the rest at lunch. The residents, too."

During the next hour, Callie's initial impression of an irate, dandelion-haired virago who waged war with innocent boxes underwent a swift reevaluation.

Despite her abrupt manner, Signora Alberti's staff appeared to adore her. The two mental-health techs, one Italian and one French. The nurse-practitioner from Corinth, Greece. The three translators who between them spoke eleven different languages. The multinational kitchen crew busy cleaning up after breakfast. Even Signora Alberti's *idiota* assistant, who turned out to be an Italian grad student working at the center as part of his hands-on training for a master's in cognitive therapy from La Sapienza, one of the oldest and most prestigious universities in Europe.

Unfortunately, the intern's English was as limited as Callie's Italian. After struggling to communicate using the impatient director as an intermediary, they agreed to compare notes at a later date. Hopefully, when they'd each gained a little more facility with the other's language.

Staff intros over, Alberti gave Callie a tour of the upper stories. The second floor contained an arts and crafts area, a library, a TV room and a series of dormitory-like bedrooms, each two bedrooms linked by a shared bath. The third floor was entirely bedrooms. All but one were occupied.

"We try to match roommates who speak the same language or at least practice the same religion," the director said. "It's not always possible, of course, but we try."

"How long do the residents stay here?"

"We've placed some in jobs and homes within a few weeks. Others…" Her shoulders lifted. "Others stay much longer."

"Can they go out? Get their nails done or go to…"

"Of course they can," Alberti snapped. "This is a shelter, yes? Not a prison."

Properly chastised, Callie was given a tour of the first-floor meeting and counseling rooms, then shown her office. It was directly across from the director's and sparsely appointed. A desk, two chairs, a metal file cabinet. Delicate sconces hinted at the house's former glory, and pale squares marked the walls where pictures or portraits must have once hung.

The director jabbed a finger at the flat-screen computer monitor sitting dead center on the desk. "We update our case files daily. All counseling sessions you have with residents, either one-on-one or in group. No excuses. No delays. Operating procedures require that we change the password once a week. When we remember," she admitted grudgingly. "This week it's Aleppo221."

"Got it."

The director tipped her chin toward a row of black binders perched atop the metal file cabinet. "Those notebooks contain our operating procedures. They're in Italian, but have been translated in English and Arabic. You need to review them along with the case files, also in Italian and English. You've got some time now. We have lunch at noon, yes? There's a group session you should sit in on at two this afternoon. And I've scheduled you to teach the beginning English class at four. It's been on hold waiting for your arrival. Can you handle that?"

"Yes, ma'am."

"Simona," she said with an irritated chop of her hand. "Call me Simona."

With so many new experiences bombarding her, Callie took the precaution of jotting down the password before she forgot it. Years of inbred caution had her reversing the digits, however. That done, she logged on and opened the oldest file.

She thought she'd seen the full spectrum of family tragedy. As she worked her way through the computerized case files, she realized she'd barely scratched the surface. Her throat got tighter as she read family histories that included everything from mass murder to honor killings to kidnapping and rape.

A number of the seventy-three women currently residing at the center had lost every living relative to war. Others had suffered pain and humiliation at the hands of vengeful husbands or fathers or brothers. Two girls barely into their teens had been sold into sexual slavery and experienced appalling degradation before escaping their captors by hiding in a dung cart.

Yet when Callie accompanied her boss to lunch, they entered a room filled with lively chatter. The meal was served buffet-style in what must have been the original owners' grand salon. The fare was hearty lamb stew fortified with green peas and couscous, the preferred drink a fragrant apple tea. The women present appeared to be primarily Middle Eastern and African, with a sprinkling of Europeans. They sat at tables of four or eight. The clusters appeared cultural for the most part, with the Muslims in modest robes and hair covered by veils or scarves, the others in more flamboyant dress.

One sat alone. Head down. Shoulders hunched. Head scarf covering her hair, her very pregnant belly evident even under her loose robe. She refused to look up even when Simona stood and called for attention. Pausing at intervals to allow the translators to keep up, the director introduced the newest member of the staff. After a flurry of smiles and welcomes in several different languages, the women got on with their lunch.

Callie waited for a lull in the director's conversation with the woman on her other side to nod discreetly at the solitary diner.

"Who's that?"

Simona followed her glance. "We call her Amal, but we don't know her real name. She washed ashore in Greece a month ago, we think from a boatload of Syrian refugees that sank off the coast. If so, she was the only survivor. She won't...or can't...tell us anything about herself or her life before she arrived here."

"Is she due soon?"

"Nikki Dukakis, our nurse-practitioner, thinks it could be within the next few weeks. We don't have facilities here for a nursery, so she'll move to another center when she leaves the hospital."

How sad, Callie thought, and how frightening it must be to give birth in a strange land surrounded by people you don't know and can't communicate with, only to be shuffled from one facility to another. She couldn't help remembering the plaster cast of the pregnant woman in Pompeii and felt a wrenching hope this mother-to-be would find a safe harbor for herself and her child.

A number of the residents came up after lunch to welcome her, some shyly, some with warm smiles. Callie then sat in on the two o'clock group session conducted by one of the mental-health techs. Despite having to work through an interpreter, the tech did a very credible job getting the women to participate.

At four o'clock Callie walked into the beginning English class feeling nervously inadequate. She soon found she didn't have to worry. The seven women and one teen in the class were eager to learn, and the teaching aids included very basic flash cards, picture books and whiteboards. The youngest class member, named

Sabeen, had a wide gap between her front teeth and seemed to take special delight in repeating sibilants like "sleep" and "snake." With each whistle, she'd giggle, slap her palm over her mouth and set the colored beads at the ends of her hundreds of tiny braids to dancing a merry tune. Having read her case file only a few hours ago, Callie could only marvel at the kidnapping victim's resilience.

Simona had indicated the staff were welcome to eat dinner with the residents, although most preferred a little separation after their long days. Night duty rotated among the paid staff and involved either sleeping at the center or remaining at home, close to a phone.

Since it was Callie's first day on the job, she opted to have dinner at the center. She shared a table with a woman from northern Iraq whose husband and three sons had been beheaded by ISIS last month. A former university professor, she spoke English and kept the conversation focused deliberately and exclusively on Callie. Where she was from. Where she'd gone to school. Why she'd come to Rome. Why the United States had invaded her country, then plunged it into chaos. Well aware she had to earn these women's trust, Callie answered as honestly as she could.

The night air was cold and brisk when she walked back to her apartment, accompanied by dark-haired, dark-eyed Nikki Dukakis. The nurse-practitioner lived only two streets over and invited Callie to have dinner the following evening with her and her husband.

"Simona is coming, too," she said. "And Carlo, if he has returned to Rome. My Dominic is with the Greek Trade Commission. He does business with Carlo, which is how I came to work at the center. But I'll do my best to keep them from talking trade embargoes all night."

She waved a cheerful goodbye at the corner, and Callie climbed the stairs to the third floor. Fumbling off her glove, she activated the scanner and let herself into the two rooms that were already beginning to feel like home. Her first order of business was a hot, steamy shower. Her second, snuggling into warm pj's. Her third and most important, calling Joe.

"Hey," she said when he picked up. "How's Zurich?"

"Cold. Snowing. Traffic pretty much at a standstill. But I got done what I needed to."

"So you're going to fly back to the States tomorrow?"

"If the airport stays open. Your turn. How was your first day?"

"Exhilarating. Exhausting. And really, really humbling. These women have been through so much, Joe. I spent most of the day waffling between a burning desire to help and questioning whether my puny skills are up to the task."

"They are. How'd you get along with *il Drago*?"

"I'm on probation until I prove I'm not just another do-gooder Carlo foisted on her. Which might be kind of tough, since I hope to do good and Carlo *did* foist me on her."

"Like I said this morning, my money's on you. Hang on, I've got another call." He returned a few seconds later. "Sorry, I need to take this. I'll call you back."

"That's okay. I'm pooped. I'll talk to you tomorrow. Good night, Joe."

"Night, Pansy Eyes."

Her voice lingered in Joe's mind as he reconnected with the caller he'd put on hold. "Yo, Frank. What's up?"

His Defense Intelligence Agency buddy didn't waste

time on chitchat. "A report just crossed my desk I think you should know about."

"I'm listening."

"Someone's been making inquiries about the place you had me check out a few days back. Very casual, very innocuous inquiries. They were buried deep in a flurry of other chatter."

"And?"

"And up until these queries surfaced, we were pretty sure we'd taken this particular someone down."

Joe's stomach went tight. "Can you give me details?"

"Not over an open line."

Joe vowed instantly to depart Zurich within the next hour, snow or no snow. If he couldn't fly out, he'd either drive or jump a high-speed train to whatever airport was still open. Once there, he'd charter an executive jet if necessary.

"I'll see you tomorrow."

He cut the connection and stood for a moment, hefting the phone in his palm. The ink had barely dried on the deal he'd cut with Callie. No wrapping her up in cotton wool. No ignoring mutually agreed-to boundaries. No unilateral decisions…except in extraordinary circumstances.

The problem was, he didn't know how extraordinary these circumstances might be. Serious enough for Frank Harden to contact him, certainly. And troubling enough for Joe to pull out all the stops to get back across the pond. Until he was in possession of some cold, hard facts, though, he couldn't see worrying Callie. Besides, this was obviously not something that could or should be discussed over the phone.

Refusing to admit he was rationalizing, he stabbed a speed-dial number and connected with the on-duty controller at his twenty-four-hour operations center. "I need out of Zurich tonight and into DC tomorrow. Any way you can work it."

"I'm on it, boss."

By the time he'd thrown his toiletries in his shaving kit and stuffed his spare clothes in his carryall, the controller called back to confirm the Zurich airport was still open.

"You're in luck. Flights look iffy for later tonight, but right now they're keeping the runway plowed and the planes deiced. I got you on Lufthansa leaving for New York in two hours and the shuttle from there to DC. You'll have to hustle to make it."

"I'll make it."

Chapter Nine

Callie got up early enough the next morning to make a quick cup of coffee. Just one, though. What she really wanted was one of those sinfully rich white-chocolate espressos at the little café she'd discovered yesterday.

The air was still crisp and cold. Bundled against the chill, she wove through the backpacking school kids and early shoppers. The scent of hot, strong coffee and fresh-baked pastries welcomed her when she ducked inside the café. While she waited for her croissant and espresso in its elegant, silver-handled glass, her gaze roamed the framed black-and-white photos. There was Sophia Loren again, and Jack Kennedy. And a helmeted general in jodhpurs and a low-slung holster.

Patton? Could that really be Patton?

Her glass in one hand and the croissant in the other, she tried to edge past the stand-up counter crowd for a closer look. She was almost there when one of the patrons closed the lid of his computer and turned to leave. She jumped back to avoid a collision but sloshed some foamy white chocolate on his sleeve.

"Oh! *Scusi!*"

The man muttered something that didn't sound too complimentary under his breath and grabbed a napkin to dab at his jacket sleeve.

"I'm sorry," Callie said in English. "I hope it didn't get in your laptop."

He jerked his head up and stared at her with unfriendly eyes. Then he turned on one heel and shouldered his way unceremoniously through the crowd.

"Ohhh…kay," she said to his back, "And no, I didn't splash hot coffee on my hand and burn myself, but thanks for asking."

Shrugging off the incident, she enjoyed the croissant and what was left of her espresso, then headed for the center.

Her second day on the job turned out to be even busier than the first. She sat in on another group therapy session at nine and attended an occupational assessment workshop at eleven. With the aid of a translator, a job placement specialist gently probed a sad-eyed, stoop-shouldered young widow for possible employment choices.

Callie joined a table of three women at lunch. Although English wasn't their native language, all three spoke it with varying degrees of proficiency. One, the victim of a vicious disfigurement by a jealous husband, hid the gaping hole where the tip of her nose had been cut off behind a veil. A native of Bangladesh, Leela had contacted an IADW outreach worker after that same loving husband had driven her out of their home with a whip.

"Simona says the doctors can fix my face," she murmured in soft, very British English. "She says she will tell Prince di Lorenzo to arrange it."

"Which he will do," one of the other women said with a smile. "He lives in fear of Simona, although he is twice her weight and so much older."

Weight, Callie agreed with. But older? Although she didn't know his for sure, she would guess the prince was somewhere in his mid-to-late thirties.

Her glance shot to the center's director seated at a table across the room. With her snowy hair and lined face, Simona certainly looked to have some years on him.

Leela followed her glance and said quietly, "She has suffered greatly, our Simona. Although she does not speak of it, it's said her hair turned white overnight."

Callie was still digesting that startling revelation when the subject of their discussion pushed away from her table and gestured for the newest member of her staff to join her. Once in the hall, the director posed a curt question.

"Are you qualified to conduct trauma therapy?"

Callie had used a trauma-focused approach with some of the children she'd worked with. Getting them to expose their memories and fears resulting from abuse or other trauma required a delicate touch, however.

"It's been a while..."

The tentative response sent an impatient flicker across the director's face. A younger face, Callie could see now, than her white hair and the deep grooves creasing her cheeks would indicate.

"Is that a yes or no?" she asked curtly.

"Yes."

"*Bene!* I want you to work with Amal. Maybe you can connect with her. God knows none of the rest of us can."

"I'll try my best."

"You do that. You do that."

Callie had to conduct an extensive search for the pregnant woman. She finally found her tucked in a corner of the second-floor arts and crafts room. She was almost completely hidden behind an artificial palm that the center's Christian residents had draped with handmade stars and silver tinsel. The small crèche under the palm reminded Callie of the purchases she'd made in Naples. She would take them out of their wrapping when she got home, she decided, and set up a little bit of Christmas in her apartment. Kate and Dawn and Tommy would just have to wait for their gifts. But first...

"Hello, Amal."

The quiet greeting startled the other woman. She whipped her head around, her dark eyes frightened, and made an instinctive move to shield the clipboard in her lap. Callie caught just a glimpse of a pencil drawing on the top sheet of the paper before the loose sleeve of Amal's robe covered it.

One glimpse was enough. With hardly more than a dozen bold strokes, the woman had masterfully interpreted the clean, fluid lines of Michelangelo's *David*.

"Oh," Callie breathed. "That's beautiful." She gestured in an attempt to overcome their language barrier. "Please, may I see it?"

Amal's arm remained firmly positioned over the sketch. The fear had left her eyes, but there was no mistaking the message they now conveyed. Ignoring the back-off signal, Callie did a quick scan of the room. The game table held a pencil and small pad for score-keeping. She grabbed both.

"I took a few art classes in school," she confessed as she dragged a chair over and positioned it next to the stone-faced woman. "Mostly art history, although I do like to draw. Unfortunately I'm not very good."

According to Simona, their best guess was that Amal had survived the tragic sinking of a refugee boat from Syria. Callie didn't know a word of Arabic. But she'd used art therapy with children many times in her previous job and knew it could cross generational barriers. She hoped it would cross language barriers, as well.

"This is me." She sketched a fairly decent female figure with longish hair. "This is where I'm from."

She added a quick backdrop of Boston's skyscrapers, although she knew each stroke was a calculated risk. The US and its allies were waging an air war in Syria. Amal's father or brothers or husband might have fought—might *still* be fighting—either with or against rebel forces. Yet everything Callie had been taught, every nugget of experience she'd gained over her years as a counselor, dictated that she lay a foundation of honesty.

"And this is you."

Flipping to a clean page, she stretched the limits of her artistic skills with a quick portrait of a figure wearing a head scarf. Then she held the sketch out to the silent woman at her side.

"Where are you from?"

Callie knew she risked alienation by pushing too hard. Possibly total and irrevocable shutdown. Yet the longer Amal hesitated, the harder Callie's heart hammered. Finally the other woman reached for the pad, but her hand trembled so violently that she snatched it back.

"It's okay," Callie said quietly. "You're safe here."

She knew Amal couldn't understand her. Knew, too, that platitudes meant little to a woman who'd lost everything. She held her breath as Amal retrieved the pad. Then slowly, so slowly, the other woman sketched a backdrop to the solitary figure.

Despite the small size of the canvas she had to work with, the layers came together in stark, minimalistic detail. Bombed buildings. Piles of rubble. Children with eyes too large for their skeletal faces. Just as slowly, she added another rendering of Michelangelo's *David*. Curly haired. Square jawed. With fierce eyes and a lethal-looking semiautomatic held waist high.

"Is this…" Callie had to stop, pull in a breath. "Is this your husband?"

Her question drew no response. The other woman stared down at the sketch for long moments. Then her pencil lashed out. Suddenly. Violently. Slashing from right to left so viciously that the paper shredded and Callie had to grab her wrist to stop the desecration.

"Amal! It's okay! You're safe here. You and your baby. You're both safe."

With a guttural sound, the other woman jerked free and thrust out of her chair. Her own sketch jammed tight against her chest, she whirled and ran out of the room.

Callie didn't go after her. She wanted to. Ached to. But training and experience kept her riveted in place. The next move—if there was one!—had to come from Amal.

Still, doubts stung like an angry swarm of wasps as she went downstairs to her office and powered up her computer. Simona's instructions had been specific. Case files were to be updated daily. No excuses, no delays. Any counseling sessions with residents, either one-on-one or in group, went in their file.

Callie curved her fingers over the keyboard while she organized her thoughts. Then entered the password, pulled up Amal's case file and battled the excruciatingly slow system to detail her failed attempt to bridge the communication gap. The entry complete, she grimaced at the flickering screen. So much for proving to Simona Alberti that she wasn't just another of Carlo's do-gooders. She logged out, wondering how long it would take before the director jumped down her throat.

Simona pigeonholed her that same evening, not long after Callie arrived at Nikki Dukakis's spacious flat.

Nikki's husband answered the door. The Greek was seriously gorgeous and wreathed in the same hot, spicy aroma that wafted from the rear of the apartment.

"I'm Dominic Dukakis," he said as he took her coat, hanging both it and her shoulder bag on an antique clothes tree in the hall. "And you must be Carlo's American."

Not quite sure how to respond to that one, she merely smiled and held out her hand. "Callie Langston."

"Come in, come in. Nicola's in the kitchen. I'll tell her you're here and fetch you a glass of wine. Or would you prefer ouzo?"

"Wine, please. Red, if you have it."

"Of course."

"Simona's here, too," he said as he gestured to a wide archway that opened onto a high-ceilinged room. "If you care to join her, I'll bring your wine."

"'Carlo's American,'" Simona echoed sardonically

when Callie joined her. "I've no doubt you'll wear that label until his next 'friend' takes your place."

"I've worn worse."

The calm reply earned a sharp look from the director, followed by a reluctant nod. "I don't doubt you have. I read your update in Amal's file," she added in a quick change of direction.

Callie braced herself, but to her surprise, the snowy-haired Simona gave her an unexpected stroke.

"You accomplished what none of us have been able to do. You connected with her."

"Only for a few moments."

"You connected," Simona repeated.

Encouraged by the unexpected praise, Callie shared her thoughts. "Amal whipped a detailed background sketch out so quickly, with such bold, sure strokes. I'm sure she's had formal training. She's that good."

"What are you thinking? That she might be an established artist?"

"Very possibly. I'm going to surf the net and see what I turn up. In the meantime, I'll try to connect with her via art again. Perhaps use it as a springboard for trauma therapy, as you recommended, or adult cognitive behavioral therapy."

Simona cocked her head, her blue eyes piercing. "You're trained in adult CBT?"

"I worked primarily with children in my last job, but I volunteered one weekend a month at the Boston VA hospital. We found CBT to be a very useful tool when working with patients suffering from post-traumatic stress."

The director glanced away. "*Sì,*" she murmured. "It can be."

Whatever she was seeing, it wasn't the impressionistic rendition of Mykonos's famous windmills that occupied a good portion of the far wall. Callie knew better than to probe. Not that she would anyway in a social setting. Instead she stood quietly until the Italian shook off her memories and deliberately changed the subject.

"We don't make Christmas a big celebration at the center, you understand."

"I would guess not, since so many of the residents are of different faiths."

"We try to accommodate those who are Christians, however. So if you have no plans for…"

"Here you are." The interruption came from Dominic, who returned with a bowl-shaped glass. "This is from the vineyard of Katogi and Strofilia, in northern Greece. Although Carlo would never agree, I think you'll find it as good—or better!—than any Italian red. And speaking of our xenophobic prince," he said as the doorbell jangled, "that will be him."

Callie could never quite pin down what it was about Carlo di Lorenzo that seemed to expand whatever room he entered. It certainly wasn't his appearance. The man was a fireplug, as wide at the middle as he was through the shoulders. What's more, his shiny bald spot had crept forward another inch or two since Callie had last seen him at Dawn and Brian's wedding. But his dark eyes danced above his luxuriant handlebar mustache, and no woman alive could remain immune to his obvious delight as he crossed the room, his hands outstretched.

"Calissa, *cara mia!*"

"Ciao, Carlo."

He took her hands in both of his and raised them to his lips with a dramatic flourish that had her smiling, Dóminic grinning and Simona rolling her eyes.

"You grow more beautiful every day, Calissa. But

this…" He dropped his gaze to her ring and twisted his lips in exaggerated sorrow. "I couldn't believe it when Joe told me that you were engaged. Surely you cannot mean to marry that block of wood. Not when I have offered to show you the delights of Marrakech and Bali."

"Her," Simona said with a small snort, "and a hundred other women."

"Ah, yes." With a spectacularly unsuccessful attempt to hide a grimace, the prince released Callie's hands and turned to face his nemesis. "Dominic told me you would be here, *il Drago*."

Callie stiffened, expecting fireworks, but Simona Alberti seemed to take the label as a tribute.

"And you still came. How very brave of you," she drawled, the sarcasm as sharp as dagger points.

He drew himself up to his full height, which put him almost at eye level with the director. He looked, Callie thought, like a mastiff going nose to nose with a whip-thin greyhound. Simona didn't appear the least intimidated, but before either of them went for the throat, Nikki strolled in from the kitchen.

"Sorry, everyone. I must confess I'm a better nurse than cook. Dominic, my darling, get Carlo a drink. And check the dolmades."

Sending her husband on his way with an airy wave, Nikki kissed Callie on both cheeks and received one of Carlo's flamboyant greetings.

"Ciao, Nicola. You're far too beautiful for that lump of Greek clay you're married to. Since I can't convince Callie to run away with me, perhaps I can talk you into abandoning Dominic and allowing me to show you the wonders of—"

"Yes, yes, we know," Simona interrupted with unconcealed irritation. "Marrakech or Bali or the South

Pole. Now, for pity's sake, may we stop this nonsense and discuss something actually important?"

"By all means," Carlo returned with soft, silky menace. "Please tell me, Madam Director, what's so important that we must dispense with civility?"

Whoa! Callie had only ever seen the prince at his most charming. This combination of haughty aristocrat and ice-edged commander made her blink and Nikki step in hastily to defuse the situation.

"It's the computers, Carlo. Simona and I were talking about them before you arrived. They're old and slow."

Callie couldn't help recalling her frustrating session just a few hours ago. "Not just the computers. The wireless router, too. The signal's so weak it takes forever to get online."

"When we can get on at all," Nikki put in.

"If I'm to submit the ridiculously detailed reports you and the board require," Simona said tartly, "I must have the tools to do it."

"*Madre di Dio!*" Palms up, Carlo surrendered with a return of his urbane smile. "How can I withstand the onslaught of three such determined women? I'll get you what you need."

The promise won delighted thank-yous from Callie and Nicola and a curt nod from Simona.

"See that you do." The brusque order wiped the smile off Carlo's face. If the director noticed his sudden scowl, however, she ignored it. "Nikki, I think I smell something burning. Shall we go help Dominic in the kitchen?"

"*Ochi!*"

Their hurried departure left Callie standing beside an obviously irate Carlo. A growl rolled up from deep

in his chest as he shot narrow-eyed darts at their re-
treating backs.

"She never allows me the last word, that one. Never!"

Callie had no trouble guessing which she he referred to.

"If she were one of my troops, I would have her up on
charges of insubordination," he steamed. "But does she
care that she shows me little respect? Does she worry
that the entire board quakes every time she comes before them? No, damn her, no. Instead, she makes me
burn to kiss that condescending smirk off her face every
time I'm with her!"

Callie jaw went slack. Mouth open, she gaped at the
furious prince and fumbled for a response. *Any* kind
of a response. Thankfully, she was saved by the bell.

The loud jangle brought Dominic's head popping out
of the kitchen door. With it came a cloud of gray smoke.

"Carlo, *aprire la porta, per favore.*"

The prince balked, obviously torn between answering
"*la porta*" and making a quick call to the fire department. He threw out a spate of urgent Italian and Dominic
returned what Callie sincerely hoped were hearty reas-
surances. Still, she decided to retrieve her phone from
the purse she'd left hanging in the hall and keep it close
at hand. Just in case. She'd taken only a few steps, however, when she got her second shock in as many minutes.

"Ciao, Giuseppe."

With a mix of surprise, confusion and pure joy, she
watched the prince greet the former chief of his special
security detail with a hearty thump on the shoulder.

"I thought you'd left Rome," di Lorenzo commented.

"I flew home last night and did a quick turnaround."

"That was indeed quick. But why would you…"

He broke off as Joe's glance shot past him and fixed
on Callie.

"Of course." The prince's mustache lifted in a wicked grin. "I would not leave her alone too long, either, were I you."

"Yeah," Joe drawled. "That was pretty much my thinking."

Callie had recovered enough to take exception to that bit of blatant chauvinism. Which she would certainly have done, if Joe hadn't sniffed the air and suddenly stiffened.

"Jesus! Is this place on fire?"

"I'm not sure," Carlo admitted. "I'll go see."

Joe took advantage of his departure to cross to where Callie stood and brush his mouth over hers. As light as the kiss was, she felt the scrape of the bristles darkening his cheeks and chin. She also took note of the red rimming his eyelids and the deep creases bracketing his mouth.

"What's happened, Joe? Why did you turn right around and fly back in Rome?"

"Not here," he said with a small shake of his head.

She didn't bother to ask how he'd known where to find her. She did, however, want to know why he hadn't held to his end of the bargain they'd negotiated a few days ago.

"How come you didn't let me know you were coming right back?"

"Check your phone."

Frowning, she dug it out of her shoulder bag and discovered it was in silent mode. She'd set it on vibrate before the therapy session she'd sat in on this morning, she now remembered, and had forgotten to take it off. She also discovered two voice mails, both from Joe, and four texts, two from him and one each from Kate and Dawn.

"You need to leave the ringer on, Callie."

"I don't want it going off during therapy sessions."

"Then keep it in your pocket, not your purse. So you'll feel it vibrate."

"Why?" she asked again. "What's going on?"

"We'll talk about it at your place. Right now we'd better..."

A wild clanging shrieked through the air. Callie winced and clapped her hands over her ears, thunking herself with the phone in the process.

"Smoke detector," Joe shouted over the din. "Open the door and some windows. I'll see what the hell's happening in the kitchen."

Stuffed grape leaves. That's what was happening. Tight little rolls filled with ground lamb, rice, chopped onion, minced garlic and fragrant spices.

Once they extinguished the fire, Nikki and Dominic and their guests discovered that one of the dolmades had somehow tipped out of the baking pan and fallen unnoticed to the back of the oven. It toasted to a blackened crisp before igniting and setting the remaining appetizers and a pan of souvlaki ablaze.

The cleanup didn't actually take all that long. Dominic drenched the charred remains in the sink, then carried both pans out to the balcony while Nikki assured anxious neighbors their homes weren't about to go up in flames. In the meantime Carlo, Joe, Simona and Callie waved dish towels to dispel the acrid smoke.

Dominic joined their effort after his trip to the balcony. Flapping a towel vigorously, he threw Joe a curious look. "Have we met?"

"Name's Russo. Joe Russo. I came to find Callie."

"Oh. Well, thanks for helping out here, Joe."

"No problem."

* * *

Fifteen minutes later their collective efforts had replaced most of the smoke with cold night air, and Nikki had been introduced to her uninvited guest. Like Dominic, she thanked Joe for coming to the rescue, then suggested they all repair to a nearby restaurant.

"We promised you dinner," she insisted. "It'll take a while yet for the apartment to totally air out, and I don't intend to turn the stove on again tonight. Maybe ever. I did mention, didn't I, that I'm a much better nurse than cook?"

"You are," Simona confirmed before adding a tart, "thank goodness."

Laughing, her husband retrieved their guests' coats and shepherded them out into the night. Still puzzled by Joe's unexpected return, Callie tucked her arm in his and asked quietly whether they should beg off dinner.

"No, this'll work. I need to talk to Carlo. I'll get him aside for a few minutes at the restaurant."

His discussion with the prince took place in a quiet corner of the bar. Callie watched them from the table in the noisier eating area, Joe's head bent close to Carlo's, the prince listening with a frown.

Both men wore neutral expressions when they rejoined the group, and Callie was forced to bridle her unease until she and Joe returned to her apartment some two hours later. She waited until they'd shed their coats and gloves and scarves, dumped some grounds in the coffeemaker and pointed to the kitchen chairs.

"Now," she demanded when they faced each other across the tiny table. "Why are you here? What's going on?"

"Someone's been making inquires about the center. Someone my contact at the Defense Intelligence Agency thought had been taken out."

"Taken out? As in…?"

"Made dead," Joe said flatly. "Bastard was driving a vehicle that took a direct hit from a drone five months ago. My contact thinks now the driver might've been someone who looked so much like the target that whoever called in the strike got it wrong."

"And this…this target is interested in the center? Why?"

"We're not sure. Best guess is because he knows one of the current residents."

That might be their best guess, but there were others. Callie knew Joe well enough now to sense he was holding back. Shielding her. Trying to protect her from the big, bad, ugly world.

"What are the other possibilities?"

"They're a stretch, Callie. Not credible threats."

"Tell me."

He didn't want to frighten her. She could see it in his eyes.

"Tell me."

He answered reluctantly. "One scenario says the women at the center have forsaken their honor by fleeing their homelands and adopting the decadent ways of the West."

"So they should be punished. As if they haven't already been punished enough," she added savagely. "What else?"

"It's the other side of the same coin. You people at the center are working a hidden agenda. In the guise of helping refugees, you're forcing them to deny their heritage, their religion."

"So *we* should be punished."

"Like I said, these scenarios are out there. Not credible."

"Credible enough for you to jump on a plane and come straight back to Rome," she pointed out.

He couldn't argue with that, and Callie couldn't believe they were actually sitting here talking about drone strikes and retaliating against helpless women who'd already suffered so much.

This was Joe's world, she thought with a fist-size knot in her throat. And now hers.

"How much did you tell Carlo?" she asked after a futile attempt to swallow the lump.

"Enough. He's going to advise the other members of the board."

"What about Simona? You have to tell her, too."

"Carlo and I plan to brief her tomorrow."

"She's not going to like this."

"Got that impression." Joe's gray eyes flickered with something she might have mistaken for amusement under other circumstances. "Funny, I've never known di Lorenzo to go six shades of pale at the mere mention of a woman's name. Your boss must put him and the rest of the board through the wringer."

Callie didn't comment. She still hadn't quite processed the prince's earlier outburst, wasn't even sure now that she'd heard him correctly.

"I thought I'd camp out here for a few days," Joe said casually. Too casually. "Or we could move to a hotel. It would give us a little more space."

She glanced around the tiny apartment with its bright yellow walls and incredible view. She hadn't put much of a personal stamp on it yet. Just angled the kitchen table so she could drink in the sight of St. Peter's dome with her morning coffee and set out the nativity figures she'd bought in Naples. They rubbed shoulders on her postage stamp of an end table. Dawn's flame-haired angel, Tommy's Disney figure, Kate's despised political candidate and the traditionally robed Joseph.

Her gaze shifted from the Virgin Mary's protector to her own. With a sense of inevitability, Callie accepted that her Joe wasn't going anywhere any time soon.

"Let's stay here."

Chapter Ten

Joe had agreed to meet Carlo at the center at eight thirty. Their plan was to beard the director in her den before the problems and events of the day distracted her or fired her temper.

He woke at his usual five o'clock and lay in the shuttered stillness, trying to shift his focus from the warm butt nested against his groin to the sparse data Frank Harden had shared.

The known aliases of the terrorist supposedly taken out by the drone strike. A list of atrocities attributed to the man as verified through human, signal, geopolitical and open-source intelligence. A blurred photo taken from a half mile away. The date, time and coordinates of the airstrike that had—supposedly—taken him out. There was nothing to suggest the bastard had survived the hit. Nothing, that was, except the recent queries about the center operated by IADW.

The probes themselves were innocuous enough.

None would've triggered an alert if not for the fact they'd been made on the same laptop previously owned by the target of the strike. A laptop that went off-line at the precise instant the drone hit. A laptop that had come back online only two days ago.

US cyberspooks had pinpointed the source of the transmissions. By triangulating cell towers and satellite systems, they'd zoomed in on a squalid, teeming tenement in Palermo, on the island of Sicily. A door-to-door search by Italian security forces hadn't yielded the laptop, however, or any indication of who might have powered it up.

Joe had his own people working the problem—his cybersecurity folks at home, Emilio Mancera here in Italy. The affable Roman had met him at the airport last night, gotten a quick briefing and put one of his own men on a flight to Palermo an hour later.

If the residents of that squalid tenement had withheld any information from the police, Emilio's man would squeeze it out of them. He knew the island, knew the inner workings of the criminal element that still flourished there. Knew, too, that the Mafia had shed its skin several times over the decades. They were still heavily into narcotics and protection rackets, of course, but now funneled their profits into legitimate businesses like shopping malls and hotels and apartment complexes…all built by a construction industry that operated on bribes, kickbacks and corruption. Without a single twinge of conscience, Joe had given the green light to apply all three if necessary.

In the meantime, he and Carlo would work the problem from this end. Starting with a thorough scrub of the backgrounds of each and every resident at the center and…

"Nmmg."

The indistinct mumble was accompanied by a twitch that sent Joe's thoughts sliding sideways. He held himself still, his breath stuck in his throat, as Callie wiggled again.

She couldn't seem to find a satisfactory position. With another mumble, she straightened one knee. Bent it again. Canted her hips. Thrust her bottom, and put Joe in an instant sweat.

"Callie. Sweetheart."

He tried to ease back a few inches. She wiggled again and locked onto him with the precision of a laser-guided heat-seeking missile. Smothering a curse, Joe shifted his head on the pillow and threw a glance at the window. His internal clock said it was still predawn. The blackened shutters confirmed that.

Hell! No way he could hold out until six or seven. Not hard and hurting like there was no tomorrow. If he and Callie hadn't ended last night with an extended tussle between the sheets, he might've rolled her over and initiated a repeat performance. But she'd collapsed on his chest, and Joe had barely found enough strength to drag up the covers before they were both out.

He'd let her sleep, he decided, and use this quiet time to contact his cybergeeks. He'd check in with Emilio, too. But not here. Somewhere that served thick, black, vein-opening coffee.

Callie was still dead to the world when he returned with two espressos and a paper sack of fresh-baked pastries. It didn't take long for the seductive aromas to penetrate her consciousness. Especially after Joe held a still-warm *cornetto* mere inches from her nose. She blinked awake, stared owlishly at the marmalade-filled bun and slicked her tongue over sleep-dry lips.

"Does that taste as good as it smells?"

"Only one way to find out."

An arm snaked out from under the blankets. Fingers latched onto the sticky sweet. Three bites later, a tousled head of mink-brown hair popped up.

"Any more where that came from?"

"On the kitchen table. Espresso, too."

He smiled as she lit up like the gaudy Christmas decorations strung across the streets outside. Rolling out of bed, she dragged a blanket around her like a tent and made for the kitchen.

"I waited for you to wake up to take a shower," he commented. "I'll make it quick."

She was too busy exploring the contents of the bag to do more than flap a distracted hand.

Joe emerged fifteen minutes later showered and shaved. Callie took considerably longer, but the results were definitely worth the wait. The steamy shower had left a delicate blush on her cheeks, and her hair fell in glossy, raisin-dark waves above a sky blue turtleneck sweater. The worry was back, though, shadowing her eyes to a purple so deep they looked almost black.

"What time did you say Carlo is going to meet us at the center?"

"Eight thirty. But it might be better if you stay out of this one."

"Why?"

"Your boss is already torqued at me for asking to review the center's screening process. Even more at Carlo for insisting it happen. No need to get her pissed at you, too."

Callie didn't comment but had to admit she was secretly happy to stay out of the line of fire.

Unfortunately, she didn't stay out of it long.

Bundled in boots, jeans, a warm sweater and her wool duster, she huddled close to Joe's side for the short walk to the center. Carlo was already there and looking none too thrilled with the task ahead.

Callie peeled off with a murmured "good luck" and headed for her office to prepare for the nine o'clock group session. When she came out twenty minutes later, notebook in hand, Simona's door was closed. The thick panel didn't quite block the sound of raised voices, though, or the thump of something banging down on the desk. Simona's palm? Carlo's fist?

She didn't stick around to find out. But when she got to the session room, the news that the mental-health tech who normally conducted this group therapy had called in sick added another wrinkle to the day. Luckily, the group was a small one. Only one translator and four participants: the two teens who'd escaped brutal sexual slavery, the disfigured wife from Bangladesh and the sad-eyed, stoop-shouldered young widow. Hiding her nervousness at being thrust into the role of facilitator as opposed to observer, Callie picked up where they'd left off yesterday.

"We were talking about how we see ourselves, and how what we've experienced colors our self-image."

She waited for the translator, then picked her way carefully over sensitive ground.

"Too often when something bad happens to us, something we can't control, we think it's our own fault. We feel guilty, anxious. Unable to make decisions or relate to others."

The woman from Bangladesh drew her veil tighter across her mutilated face and murmured something Callie couldn't quite catch.

"I'm sorry. What did you say?"

"A leper," Leela said in her soft, British-accented English. "I feel like a leper. I show myself to no one."

The thinner of the two teens spoke next. A single word, muted, reluctant.

"Unclean," the interpreter translated. "After what was done to her, she feels unclean."

Callie nodded and looked to the other two participants. The young widow shrank back against her chair and shook her head, but the second teen, the one named Sabeen, chose to speak out. Usually so happy and giggly, she launched into an angry spate that set the beads at the ends of her braids dancing and the words whistling through the gap in her front teeth.

"She, too, feels dirty," the interpreter related, hurrying to keep. "She bathes two or three times a day but cannot wash the smell of those pigs off her skin, out of her hair."

As if to emphasize her feelings, the girl grabbed a fistful of the braids and shook them angrily.

"Sabeen says she would cut them off. All of them. As she would cut off the thing between the legs of every man who took her."

"Well…"

Callie was treading delicate ground here. For all she knew, those colorful beads denoted rank or marital status in the tribe these girls had been abducted from. They'd chosen not to return to their tribe, however, deciding instead to make a tortuous journey to another country, another way of life.

"Why *not* cut them off?" she asked gently. "The

braids, I mean. Although I think castrating the pigs who hurt her is a pretty good idea, too."

The question was obviously one the girl had debated before. A host of emotions flickered across her face, not least of which was fear of losing the last vestige of her identity in this foreign world.

Callie waged a similar internal debate. She was here to facilitate, not direct. Enable, not lead. Yet she couldn't force herself to remain detached and neutral and merely nurturing. Something drove her to bridge the seeming impossible gulf between these women's world and her own.

"Hang tight," she instructed through the interpreter. "I'll be right back."

She hurried down the hall to her office, throwing a quick glance at Simona's closed door as she went. She didn't hear any raised voices or loud thumps and couldn't decide whether that was a good or bad omen. Joe could be pretty intimidating when he wanted to, she knew. Carlo, too, as she'd discovered last night. Simona would have to be made of kryptonite to stand up to both of them. And after having known the director for all of two days and a few hours, her money was on the director.

Once in her office, Callie riffled through her desk drawer for a pair of scissors. She found them in a bottom drawer, then rooted around in her purse for her handy-dandy little travel mirror. Clutching both objects, she hurried back to the session room.

"I haven't suffered as you have," she told the other women through the translator. "I haven't experienced anything that could even remotely compare to what you've suffered. But, like you, I'm beginning a new life in a new place. So I think… No, I *know*. I'm ready for a new me."

Brandishing the scissors, she held the mirror at arm's length and tried unsuccessfully to wield the scissors with the other.

"I could use some help here. Will someone please hold the mirror for me?"

The interpreter looked as hesitant as the four residents. When none of them replied, Callie dropped the mirror, grabbed a hank of her hair, and hacked off a good eight inches.

Leela sprang to her feet, half laughing, half scandalized. "Buddha preserve us!"

Her veil slipped, revealing a glimpse of her horrific disfigurement, before she threw the ends over her shoulder again and grabbed the scissors.

"I will do it. But only if you really wish me to."

"Whack away," Callie instructed cheerfully.

Within a remarkable short period of time, hair lay in heaps on the floor. Callie's dark brown. Sabeen's black braids. Leela's hennaed tresses.

Sabeen kept slapping her hand over her mouth to contain her giggles, but her infectious laughter soon drew a half dozen curious residents. Then Nikki. Then an obviously irritated Simona.

"What goes on here?"

"Hair therapy."

Grinning, Callie shook her short, surprisingly curly locks. She felt pounds lighter and thought she looked like a completely different person. Unfortunately, her boss wasn't impressed.

"*Hair* therapy? Is that some new American fad?"

The scorn behind the question cut as sharp and as

deep as the words themselves. Smiles slipped. Expressions turned worried. Sabeen passed a nervous palm over her new buzz cut.

"It's hardly a fad." Callie's response was cool and level. "You might want to read Dr. Elaine Boyer Barrington's *Adaptive Therapies for Female Adolescents*. Her work merely reinforces the basic fact that a teenager's hairstyle is one of the most obvious indicators of her feeling of self-worth. So obvious, in fact, that therapists too often fail to ascribe it the significance they should."

Simona's brows snapped together, but she didn't challenge Callie in front of the others. Instead, she merely glowered and issued a terse command.

"I want to speak with you. In my office."

"Of course. I'll just sweep up the hair and…"

"We'll take care of it," the translator said quickly.

"Thanks."

With a smile and another toss of her short, who-would've-guessed-it curls, Callie followed her boss. Simona marched down the hall, her back stiff and her chin held at a combative angle.

"Adaptive therapies?" she huffed. "Dr. Elaine whoever Barrington? If I go online and do a search, will I find either?"

"I'd be very surprised."

"So you invented all that nonsense?"

"No, I didn't. I knew Elaine in grad school. She was a very innovative thinker but switched careers after earning her PhD. Last I heard, she and her husband were operating a treetop guest lodge in Tanzania."

Simona stopped with one hand on the doorknob of her office. Blue fire shot from her eyes. "Are you playing with me? If you are, I'll tell you now I'm not in the mood for it."

No kidding. Didn't take a genius to see her meeting with Carlo and Joe hadn't gone well and Callie was about to take the heat for it.

"Well," she said with a calm smile, "the treetop lodge might be in Zimbabwe."

Those blue lasers narrowed dangerously. Callie kept her smile in place but felt the narrowness of her escape when the director whirled and thrust open the door. She stomped in, waited for Callie to follow, then slammed it shut and wasted no time on preliminaries.

"The prince and your fiancé shared some disturbing news."

"Joe told me about it last night."

Simona resorted to the classic Italian gesture. Bringing the fingertips of one hand together, she waved it up and down. Despite her short time in Rome, Callie had seen the gesture often enough to know the most polite interpretation was *What the hell?*

"I cannot not believe this. My center, the target of inquiries by a dead terrorist! It is not to be believed."

Her accent thickened with each word, along with her indignation.

"I think," Callie replied carefully, "that we should trust Joe's instincts."

"The prince most certainly does," her boss huffed. "He informs me—*informs* me, you understand—that your Joe considers our security totally inadequate."

Callie couldn't help thinking of the rusted panel beside the front door. "Well…"

"The prince also informs me," Simona fumed, "that your fiancé sends one of his subordinates to install additional equipment."

Emilio Mancera, Callie guessed, Joe's very efficient head of operations here in Rome.

"I don't see why you would object to a little additional security," she said cautiously.

"Ha! You see no problem?" Bristling from the ends of her superfine white hair to the tip of her indignantly quivering nose, Simona folded her arms across her chest. "Then perhaps you agree that Carlo and your fiancé should have access to our case files."

"What?"

"Ah. So you didn't know?" The director assumed an expression of fake surprise. "Your fiancé didn't tell you that he wants to sit down with us? To go through every case file?"

"No, he did not."

Callie was more indignant than she'd been in longer than she could remember. At Joe, for not discussing this with her before springing it on her boss. At Simona, for thinking she would condone such a breach of ethics.

"And if he *had* discussed it with me," she added icily, "I would've given him the same answer I suspect you did."

Her obvious ire defused some of the director's. Simona's chin lost its pugnacious thrust and a satisfied smirk replaced her fake surprise.

"But, yes! I told him, '*Non lasciatevi la porta si colpisce nel culo sulla via d'uscita.*'"

Callie had picked up enough Italian to string "*porta*" and "*uscita*" together. "I got it. You told him not to let the door hit him in the ass on his way out."

"*Sì!*"

She bit her lip. She wasn't ready to let go of her indignation just yet, but the thought of this tiny sprite of a woman unceremoniously booting Joe out of her office shaved off some of its sharp edge.

"Well," she admitted after a moment, "I probably wouldn't have given him that exact answer. But close enough."

"Are you sure, Calissa? You really feel this way?"

"For pity's sake, Simona…"

"Do not fire up at me! Carlo and your bedmate have given me enough grief."

"Our intake interviews and case files are privileged information. Carlo must know that. Joe, too."

He had to. He couldn't have been in the security business without smacking up against privacy laws. Although… With an inner grimace, Callie shoved the suspicion that he might've found a way around, over or under a few of those rules and regulations to the back of her mind.

"Carlo does indeed know it," Simona confirmed, "but he says he will take the matter to the board. We will soon be caught in the middle of a fight."

"It won't be my first time."

"Yes?" The director cocked her head. "You've battled with this fiancé of yours before?"

"We've had a few differences," Callie conceded, "but we sat down and discussed them like rational adults. We'll do the same in this instance, too."

"Ha!"

"We will! But…" she said, coming off her haughty stand, "perhaps I'd better take another look at our operating procedures. I read through them my first morning, but I want to be sure I didn't lose anything in translation."

She was thoroughly acquainted with the standards of patient confidentiality as detailed in the American

Psychological Association's code of ethics, of course. She could also quote title and chapter of Massachusetts law that codified those standards. Her initial review of the center's operating procedures had indicated that IADW's policies mirrored APA's. Basically, client information and records of therapy sessions were confidential, with several internationally recognized exceptions.

One of those exceptions involved any reasonable suspicion of child abuse. Callie was intimately familiar with that provision. She'd had to exercise it far too often while acting as an ombudsman for children caught between warring parents or kids seemingly lost in the foster care system.

Belief that a client will harm himself or someone else was another exception to confidentiality laws. Callie had been forced to exercise that option on several occasions, as well.

She hadn't worked as much with the criteria involving lawsuits and court-mandated therapy sessions, however, and would have to dig deeper to make sure she fully understood IADW's position on each of them.

Crossing the hall to her own office, she retrieved one of the dusty black binders from atop the metal file cabinet. She still had her nose buried in the notebook some thirty minutes later when the sound of footsteps outside her door brought her head up. Expecting Simona, she blinked in surprise.

"Joe! I didn't hear the bell. How'd you get in?"

"Please." He gave her a pained look. "Tommy Ellis could pick the lock on the front door blindfolded. The one on the back door's even worse."

"Simona told me you'd decided to beef up our security."

"Just met with Emilio. He'll purchase the equipment and install it himself. What'd you do to your hair?"

She'd forgotten all about her new do. Lifting a hand, she combed her fingers through the curls. "I call it adaptive therapy. Like it?"

"Yeah, I do. Makes your eyes look even bigger. And speaking of therapy…" He wedged into the narrow space in front of her desk and claimed one of the two chairs. "I expect Simona also told you that she stonewalled Carlo and me a while ago."

"She told me you wanted access to our case files. She also said she, quite correctly, refused."

"Correctly?"

"Those files contain privileged information, Joe. You know that."

"They also contain intake interviews that document your residents' nationality and where they entered the refugee aid system. One of those interviews might reveal a link to the drone strike."

"Not every resident's home of origin is documented," Callie countered, thinking of Amal's shrouded past. "And even if that information *is* in the record, it's protected. We couldn't disclose it without the written consent of the individuals involved."

"So get their consent."

He said it so coolly. So matter-of-factly. As though extracting information was a matter of time, patience and technique, not ethics. A little shocked, Callie pressed him to understand.

"Joe, please. Listen to me. Most of these women have been severely traumatized. Simona, Nikki, the professionals here at the center…they've worked with them for weeks and in some cases months. I'm just beginning to make a few tentative connections. Yesterday, with a sketch pad. Today with this."

Her hand went to her hair again. Raking the shaggy curls. Standing them on end.

"I have to earn their trust, Joe. That won't happen if I ask them to sign a document they may not understand. One that strips them of the little privacy and dignity they have left."

He studied her through eyes that had gone as opaque and as impenetrable as the fog that rolled in across Boston Bay.

"What about our connection?" he asked after a long moment. "Our trust? You don't believe I could protect their privacy and dignity?"

She flinched and searched for a possible compromise, however shaky.

"Let me talk to Simona."

He nodded. Once. A brief dip of his chin. Then he pushed out of the chair. "You do that. And tell her Emilio should be here before noon."

"Wait! Where are you going?"

"I've got some business to take care of. I'll see you later."

Chapter Eleven

Joe labeled it a strategy session. Carlo, still smarting from the wounds he'd received during the morning's firefight with Simona, declared it a war council. Dominic Dukakis thought he'd been invited to the prince's palatial apartment on Via Zanardelli to discuss yet another proposed amendment to the hotly debated Greece-Italy pipeline.

He learned otherwise shortly after the three men gathered around a burled walnut table in the library. Leatherbound first editions lined the shelves that ran the length of two walls. Gilt-framed portraits of Carlo's ancestors covered every square inch of a third. The fourth boasted velvet-draped windows that give an unobstructed view of the Pantheon's colonnaded portico. None of the three men were interested in Emperor Hadrian's architectural gem, however.

When Joe explained the reason for the meeting to

Dominic, the Greek diplomat didn't bother debating the nebulous nature of the threat. Desperate refugees were wading ashore in his county by the thousands. Most carried with them hope for a better life. No small few, Dominic knew, carried a buried—sometimes burning— resentment toward the Western nations that had bombed or strafed in the ceaseless battle against terrorists. That one of those terrorists might have survived a direct strike and was now making inquiries about the center where Nicola Dukakis worked was all her husband needed to know.

He also didn't waste time sympathizing when Carlo related Simona's flat refusal to grant access to the center's computerized case files. His wife was a highly skilled nurse-practitioner, licensed to diagnose and treat in Greece, Macedonia and Italy. Dominic was well aware of the laws governing patient privacy and the confidentiality of medical records. Instead of railing at the system, he wanted to know what had to be done to protect the women who lived and worked at the center, his wife included.

"Emilio's there now," Joe reported. "He's installing new electronic locks with touch pads and putting motion detectors on the ground-floor windows."

Shuffling through a stack of papers, he extracted a schematic detailing all three floors of the center's interior and exterior.

"We're also installing surveillance cameras that feed to our twenty-four-hour monitoring service. Here, here, here and here."

Dominic's brows winged up. "Simona's fiercely protective of the residents' privacy. I'm surprised she consented to cameras, much less to twenty-four-hour monitoring."

"She agreed to exterior surveillance only." Joe shot Carlo a quick look. "But we're adding unobtrusive interior cameras that can be activated with the flick of a remote switch."

"By unobtrusive I assume you mean hidden."

"Correct."

"And you haven't told Simona about them?"

"Not yet."

The Greek blew a soundless whistle. "I sincerely hope I'm not in the line of fire when she discovers what you've done."

"She won't. Not with Emilio doing the installing."

"You live dangerously, my friend."

"Comes with the territory."

"Speaking of your man Emilio," Carlo put in. "Did he hear from *his* man in Palermo?"

"He did," Joe reported grimly. "His guy squeezed every contact, legitimate or otherwise, but got nothing. Whoever powered up that laptop knows how to cover his tracks."

Carlo muttered a curse while Joe shuffled the papers again and slid one across the table.

"This is a copy of the center's daily schedule. Also a list of outings planned for the next two weeks. I'll have someone shadowing each outing."

The list ran the gamut from shopping excursions to a walking tour of streets lit with holiday lights to attendance by three of the center's Christian residents at the pope's traditional Christmas Eve Mass.

"*Christós,*" Dominic muttered when his gaze snagged on the last item. "Fifty or sixty thousand people jam into St. Peter's Basilica for that Mass. Another four hundred thousand fill the square outside to watch it on huge screens. Your men will have a time keeping watch on these three."

"They'll manage."

Carlo picked up from there. "I spoke to a contact at *Questura Centrale*. He agreed to step up patrols by uniformed police in the area around the center. I've also briefed the commander of the ROS."

The *Raggruppamento Operativo Speciale*, or Special Operations Group, was an elite arm of Italy's national military police, specifically established to combat terrorism and organized crime.

Dominic nodded his approval of these measures and voiced a key question. "What can I do?"

"The same thing Joe and I intend to do. Become more involved in center activities. For the next few weeks, at least."

"That may not be easy to pull off," Dominic said slowly. "Some of those women have been severely traumatized by the very men who should have protected them. Nikki understands this. Simona even more so. She allows only three men to work at the center, two cooks and one mental health tech, and Nikki says she personally vetted each of them."

"Which is why it must be the three of us," Carlo responded. "*Il Drago* can hardly object to a casual visit by Nikki's husband or Callie's fiancé. Or," he added with a twist of his lips, "the chairman of the board she supposedly reports to."

Dominic looked skeptical but withheld comment as a phone pinged. All three men instinctively checked their devices, but the text message was for Joe.

"Emilio's almost done," he reported, pushing back his chair. "I'll use checking his work as an excuse for another foray into the dragon's den."

* * *

He activate the override code on the shiny new touch pad Emilio had installed beside the front door but took care to announce his arrival by texting Callie. Her answering text was short and succinct.

I'm in session. Wait in my office.

Another text pinpointed Emilio's location. Joe found his subordinate crouched beside a low sill in a small storage room at the end of the first-floor hall. Its single window was almost obscured by stacked boxes and metal shelves jammed with an assortment of office supplies. Muttering to himself, Emilio scraped at what was probably three or four centuries of paint with a sharp-edged knife.

"These windows," he snarled to Joe in idiomatic Italian, "they're a bitch."

"Need help?"

"No, this is the last. But I could use some mineral water. Or better yet, a stiff shot of grappa."

Joe was more than happy to comply with the first request. It gave him an excuse to conduct a visual surveillance of the kitchen. He'd already studied its floor plan and assessed every possible ingress and egress point. Still, nothing compared to direct eyeballing.

The unmistakable aromas of Italy hit him the moment he pushed through the swinging door. Garlic, olive oil and the sweet, heavy cream of fettuccine Alfredo. Both of the regular cooks on the center's list of employees were present. One was busy grating fresh Romano while his associate stirred several steaming pots. When Joe asked for mineral water, the stirrer merely stabbed the tip of his spoon in the direction of a stainless steel refrigerator.

Once every nook and cranny was imprinted in his mind, Joe made his way back down the hall. A quick glance in Callie's empty office confirmed she hadn't finished her therapy session. Simona's office across the hall also stood vacant. But when Joe approached the storage room at the end of the hall, Emilio's tense voice stopped him in his tracks.

The Roman tried Italian first. Then French. Then English. Each iteration was more pleading than the last. "It's okay. It's okay. Please! Don't do anything rash."

Every instinct on red alert, Joe dropped into a crouch. He shifted the water bottle to his left hand and dropped his right to the lightweight Ruger nested in its ankle holster.

"I see what you want," Emilio said. "No! It's okay! It's okay! You do it. Take my knife. Go ahead, take it."

Joe was still in a crouch, still strung wire tight, when he caught the soft thud of footsteps on the stairs at the far end of the hall. He spun around and spotted Callie frozen halfway down the spiral staircase, her eyes wide and questioning.

He put a finger to his lips. She got the message, but only to the extent of creeping down the remaining stairs on tiptoe. Cursing under his breath, Joe signaled for her to stay the hell back.

She froze in place again, her entire body rigid as she, too, caught the faint whisper of what Joe guessed was a naked blade slashing through cardboard. Emilio's voice followed a few second later.

"There. Take as much as you want." A pause, a gentler tone. "When's your baby due?"

Oh, God, Callie thought. That was Amal in there

with Emilio. Amal, who never spoke a word but could sketch like this century's answer to Michelangelo. Amal, who might give birth any day, surrounded by strangers. Callie knew she should intervene. Should let the other woman know she wasn't...

"My name's Emilio."

She held her breath as Joe's associate waited a beat. Two. Three.

"And you?" he said softly. "What's your name?"

The tableau played out in vivid high definition inside Callie's head. The dusty storage room. The impossibly handsome Roman with his buffed-up biceps and bedroom eyes. The pregnant refugee who'd lost everything. She'd just decided to terminate the agonizing inquisition when she caught a whisper so faint she almost missed it.

"They...they call me Amal."

Callie couldn't move, couldn't breathe. Astounded, unbelieving, thrilled, she locked on Joe. He transmitted an unmistakable signal to keep silent as Emilio spun out the tenuous thread.

"Amal? That's a pretty name."

Painful seconds ticked by. Callie had almost given up hope when Amal answered in tortured whisper.

"The name is a mockery."

"Why?"

The reply was low, tortured. "In Arabic it means 'hope.' But I have none."

"Why?" Emilio asked again.

So calm. So unthreatening. Yet the single word provoked a fierce response.

"You could not understand!"

"Then tell me. Explain why you're so frightened."

Callie inched closer to Joe. She felt like a world-class voyeur but wasn't about to interrupt this fragile conversation. To her intense disappointment, it was terminated a moment later.

Amal burst out of the storage room. Her robe flattening against her distended belly, she flew past Callie and Joe. Emilio emerged almost on her heels. His handsome face contorted into a scowl as he watched her rush up the spiral staircase.

"She shouldn't run like that. She could trip," he worried. "Hurt herself or the baby."

"What was that about?" Joe demanded. "What was she doing in the storage room?"

"I'll show you." Emilio went back into the dusty storage room and returned a moment later with a still-wrapped ream of copy paper.

"Here. This is what she was after." His glance cut to Callie. "She seemed desperate for it. Why don't you take it to her?"

She knew where to look this time. As she'd anticipated, Amal had taken refuge in the corner half-hidden by the potted palm with its mantle of tinsel and silver balls.

Once again Callie signaled her presence with a soft hello. And once again the mother-to-be looked up with wide eyes and refused to return her greeting.

"Emilio…the man downstairs…he said this is what you wanted."

Callie placed the ream on the table beside Amal. Despite the other woman's blank-eyed stare, a dull red crept into her cheeks.

"You know you can have as much paper to draw with as you wish. You've only to ask."

The red deepened.

"I heard you downstairs," Callie continued gently.

"You and Emilio. I'm so glad you speak English. I've been wanting to tell you something."

That produced not much as a flicker of response but she refused to give up.

"I'm completely in awe of your artistic ability," she told the other woman. "Perhaps…perhaps we could visit some of Rome's museums together. The Borghese and the Sistine Chapel top my list."

Amal's lashes swept down, but not before Callie caught the spark that leaped in her dark eyes. Hiding her own excitement, she took that for a yes.

"The Sistine Chapel might be tough to get into this close to Christmas," she said in a deliberately conversational tone. "So many tourists here for the holidays. Why don't I go online and see if I can get us tickets for the Borghese?"

She did a quick mental shuffle of her schedule. "How about tomorrow? I'll talk to Simona and see if I can move the English class to one o'clock instead of four."

She waited a few beats. "Amal? I won't push if you don't want to go. Just tell me yes or no."

The nod was short and excruciatingly slow in coming.

"Great!" Excitement shooting through her, Callie wasn't about to give the other woman time to change her mind. "I'll go downstairs right now and check on tickets."

Joe and Emilio were still in the hall. They were deep in conversation but broke off as she approached.

"Is Amal all right?" the Roman asked with concern stamped across his face.

"She's fine. I can't believe you got her to speak to you. That's the first time she's verbally communicated with anyone."

Callie wanted to kiss him. Almost did.

"You cracked the door, Emilio, and I squeezed through after you. Amal agreed to go to the Borghese with me tomorrow afternoon. I'm going online now to see if I can reserve two tickets."

"Make it three," Joe said. "I'll go with you."

"Four," Emilio put in.

Callie hesitated. "I'm not sure that's a good idea. I barely got her to agree to go with me."

"Reserve four," Joe instructed. "If she balks at an escort, Emilio and I will keep our distance. Neither of you will see us in the crowd."

"And if there is a problem with tickets," his associate added, "my cousin's wife's brother works at the museum. He'll get us in."

Callie didn't have to resort to Emilio's relatives. She reserved four tickets for a 2:30 p.m. entrance time. She also printed out the brochure containing a map and description of the exhibit rooms and took it upstairs.

"We're all set," she told Amal. "I hope you're as excited as I am."

The gleam in the other woman's eyes was answer enough. Callie prayed that including an escort wouldn't kill it.

"Is it okay if my fiancé comes with us?" she asked. "And Emilio, the man you met downstairs. When I told them what we were planning, they both said they'd like to go."

She felt a little guilty withholding the fact that neither man was driven by a burning desire to view the Borghese's art treasures. Not guilty enough to explain the reasons for their presence, however. Primarily because Joe stressed that the precise details of the drone strike were still classified. Secondarily because Simona had yet to advise Callie on how much or how little to tell the residents.

She saw the reluctance in Amal's face and moved quickly to counter it. "That's okay. They don't have to come with us."

They'd trail along behind instead.

Callie's guilt kicked up another notch. Her professional conscience pinging, she realized she couldn't keep shading the truth like this. She'd destroy her tentative connection with this woman before it even took root.

She'd just decided to cancel the outing, or at least delay it until the security scare was over, when Amal finally communicated verbally.

"The one downstairs," she whispered in a low voice.

"Emilio?"

"He has a kind face."

That wasn't how most women would see it, Callie thought in surprise. With his melting brown eyes, noble nose and sensual mouth, Emilio Mancera was a Roman god come to life. But the fact that Amal had at last deigned to speak with her thrilled Callie so much that she instantly agreed.

"Very kind. So it's all right if he joins us? He and my fiancé?"

Amal nodded.

"Okay!" Feeling as though she'd just scaled a ten-thousand-foot mountain, she shoved the brochure she'd printed at Amal. "Here's a brochure of the museum. You can study the layout before we go tomorrow. And I checked. They have wheelchairs available if you get too tired or the baby starts to weigh you down."

The other woman's hand dropped to her swollen belly. She hesitated for long moments before revealing the first hint of her past. "We walked for many days, my babe and I. Many nights. We do not need a wheelchair."

Callie couldn't help thinking of Joe's thwarted request to review the residents' intake interviews and case files. She came close, so close, to asking Amal where she'd walked *from*. And who she'd left behind.

She resisted the urge. First, because anything Amal shared with her would still be considered privileged information. Second, because Callie's instincts warned her not to push too hard, too fast.

"Okay," she said instead, "no wheelchair. We'd better take a taxi to the museum, though. You and the baby may be able to walk that far. I can't."

Once back downstairs she confirmed arrangements with Joe and Emilio and left them to finish whatever security improvements they had left while she updated Amal's case file. That done, she braced herself to brief Simona on the breakthrough, as tentative as it was.

As she suspected, the director had yet to fully recover from her contentious meeting with Carlo and Joe. When Callie tapped on her door, she snapped out a "Come in," and looked up to give her deputy a decidedly unfriendly glare.

"Have you seen these locks your fiancé's installed?" she fumed. "They read palm prints."

"I know," Callie responded. "He had one installed at my apartment, too."

The pencil Simona was balancing between two fingers seesawed back and forth, hitting the desk repeatedly. Tap. Tap. Tap. Each tap louder and angrier than the last.

"So tell me," she demanded. "What's to stop this 'security expert' you're engaged to from running these prints through various international databases?"

"I asked him about that."

The pencil hit the desk again. Faster. Harder.

"Did you? And what did he say?"

"The same thing he and Carlo told you this morning. Any prints provided voluntarily outside a therapy session aren't protected by client-counselor confidentiality."

"Perhaps not," Simona fired back. "But running these voluntarily provided prints without their owners' consent violates their privacy."

"You'll have to argue that with Carlo. Joe said the prince got a legal opinion on the matter."

"Oh, yes," Simona huffed. "He did. From one of the half dozen judges he has tucked in his back pocket. One who apparently thinks the safety and security of the masses override our residents' rights to privacy."

After almost witnessing the Boston Marathon bombing firsthand, Callie's own feelings were too contradictory to argue the point.

"Actually," she said instead, "I came in to tell you about Amal."

"What about her?"

As she described the incident with the ream of paper and the subsequent proposal to visit the Borghese, the director's angry pencil stilled.

"And she agreed to go with you?" Simona asked incredulously.

"She did." Callie couldn't help grinning. "I booked tickets for two thirty tomorrow afternoon. Assuming you don't mind me moving the English class up to one p.m., that is."

"Of course not."

To her relief, her boss relaxed into a smile. The result was a Simona Alberti that looked years younger.

Young enough, Callie thought with an inner grin, to have snared the reluctant interest of Italy's playboy prince.

"You've gotten more from Amal in a few days than the rest of us have in a month," Simona said.

"I can't claim all the credit. Emilio coaxed her into talking to him. That broke the ice."

"This fellow, Emilio. What do you know about him?"

"Nothing other than the fact that he works for Joe."

"Are you sure it's wise to include both men in this trip to the Borghese?"

"Amal seemed okay with it."

"Don't forget that drawing you told me about. The one she destroyed. The male figure in that sketch may well represent someone she fears."

"Or hates," Callie agreed, remembering how viciously she'd slashed the drawing.

"Whatever the emotion is, it's obviously very close to the surface. Be careful you don't unintentionally trigger it."

Callie took the warning to heart but could only hope an excursion to one of Rome's most famous museums would trigger joy, not hate or fear.

Joe spent the afternoon helping scan the staff and residents' palm prints into the electronic keypads Emilio had installed at the front and back entrances. Per Simona's strict orders, they made sure everyone understood they could use the palm pad or punch in an override code. Since the code consisted of sixteen alpha and numeric digits, neither Joe nor Emilio was surprised every resident went with option A.

Joe disappeared for a while after the key pads were up and running but was waiting in the little café across the street when Callie left work that evening. He noted with approval that she'd dressed for the December night in her long duster, a warm scarf and gloves. After a quick exchange with the man sharing his table, he dodged the traffic and joined her.

"Who's that?" she asked with a glance at his companion.

"One of Emilio's crew. Are you up for a walk?"

"Sure. Where to?"

"Via Condotti. We've both been cooped up all day. I thought you might like to stretch your legs and see the shops all decked out in lights."

And Joe needed to buy her a Christmas present. With everything else going on the past few days, it had almost slipped his mind.

"Ooh!" She breathed a delighted puff into the frosty air. "I've been dying to see Via Condotti. When Kate researched our trip this fall, she told us it's *the* street for high-end shopping. We couldn't afford to buy anything in those absurdly expensive boutiques, but we'd planned to cruise them anyway."

That sealed it. Her present would most definitely come from Via Condotti.

"And at Christmastime," she related in delight, "the window decorations are supposed to be spectacular."

Not just the window decorations, they soon discovered. The entire street was festooned for the holidays. Monster chandeliers of twinkling white lights illuminated the thoroughfare from the foot of the Spanish Steps to its intersection with Via del Corso. Shops touting names like Prada and Gucci and Valentino all tried to outdo each other with spectacular displays. But Joe and Callie both agreed Fendi took the prize.

A wide band of blue lights belted the Italian designer's four-story building. As if that wasn't eye-catching enough, the Fendi's signature logo sparkled in the white lights that comprised the belt's massive buckle. Like icing on an extravagant cake, the largest tree Joe had ever seen dominated the traffic circle in front of the store.

"Wait!" Callie dragged him to a halt and yanked her cell phone out of her purse, then stretched out her arm. "I have to send a selfie of us to Kate and Dawn."

Joe flinched. Years as a Delta Force operative had conditioned him to shy away from having his picture taken. His instinctive aversion had ramped up since Curaçao. He didn't need a visual reminder of that failed mission. Not when he could see one every time he looked in the mirror.

"I'll take the picture," he told Callie. "You don't need me in it."

"Yes, I do! Dawn and Kate were so bummed we wouldn't be together at Christmas. It's the first time since we were kids." She waved an arm at the glittering display. "I want them to see you and me together, enjoying all this."

"You've shared *every* Christmas since you were kids?"

"It's not all that hard to pull off when you grow up in the same small town," she retorted. "Hold still."

Okay. He could pose for one shot. For Callie. Still, he angled his head to hide the scar as she stiff-armed the phone. Her reach wasn't long enough. She barely caught the two of them in the frame, much less the lights.

"Let me do it."

He cradled her against his chest and framed them against both the tree and the belted building.

"Oh," she enthused. "That's better."

It was. Much better, Joe agreed. He had Callie in his arms and Rome lit like a Christmas tree behind him. Any thought of Curaçao faded. So did the worry that had goaded him like a vicious spur since Frank Harden's call. For the first time, Joe felt the joy of the season seep into his bones.

He took the shot, then Callie twisted in his arms.

"Take another."

She pushed up on her toes. Her arms hooked around his neck. Her mouth went from cool to hot as it molded his. With his arm still extended, Joe could only hope he would hit the right button on the camera app as he hooked his other arm around her waist and tugged her against him.

The applause pulled them apart. That, and a laughing suggestion from some men who'd stopped to watch the show. Luckily, the suggestion was in Italian. When Joe responded with a grin and lowered his arm, Callie grabbed the phone and switched immediately from camera to photo mode.

"Oh, my God! These are great. Look at that tree. And the Fendi belt! Hold on, I have to send the pics to Dawn and Kate."

Her thumbs flew. When she'd finished, he took her elbow and steered her toward the store entrance. Once again she dragged him to a halt.

"Joe! I can't afford anything in there."

"I can."

"We talked about this. Remember? I want to pay my own way."

"Christmas presents aren't part of that agreement."

"Maybe not. But I'm not into designer bags or belts or boots. Tell you what," she said when he started to protest. "You can buy me a print at the Borghese tomorrow. Something pretty I can frame and hang on my bright yellow walls."

He gave in, but only because he was already considering another gift...which turned out to be a smart move, because they never made it to the Borghese.

Chapter Twelve

The other half of her bed was empty when Callie blinked awake the next morning. She groped for her phone and peered owlishly at the digital display. Ugh! Six fifteen. Her alarm wouldn't go off for another forty-five minutes. She snuggled under the duvet again but couldn't go back to sleep. The stillness in her tiny apartment was too loud.

"Joe?"

No answer. Not that she'd expected one. She stretched lazily and wondered how in the world the man could slide out of bed, shower and/or shave, dress and depart without making normal human sounds.

Giving up the battle after a few more minutes of snooze time, she stuffed her feet into slippers and wrapped the duvet around her like a tent. When she padded into the kitchen area, she found a note propped against a large takeout coffee and a paper sack containing fresh ricotta-filled pastries.

"Bless you," she muttered as she pried the lid off the coffee and scanned the note. Surprise, surprise. Joe had some business to take care of.

She hitched up the duvet and carried the coffee back to the bedroom with her. In what was sure to become a daily habit, she ducked out on the tiny balcony to get her daily fix of the view. Night still shrouded the city, but the sky to the east showed streaks of purple and red. She still couldn't quite believe she was standing here, suspended above the rooftops of Rome and gawking at St. Peter's softly illuminated dome in the distance.

The frosty air drove her back inside. That, and the urge to take another look at last night's selfie. Plunking down on the side of the bed, she traded the coffee for her phone and scrolled through the photos she'd taken in the past week. As much as she missed Kate and Dawn, her Christmas season was turning out to be truly magical. Sharing Saint Lucia's day with the Audis. Mingling with the throng in Naples's street of the crèches. Last night's stroll through Via Condotti with its amazing display of lights.

She lingered over the selfie and had to smile at how Joe had positioned her in the shelter of his arms. Always the protector. Always the guardian.

Good thing they'd established boundaries this early in their relationship. Without those boundaries Callie knew it would be all too easy to succumb to the seductive promise of being petted and pampered. Now if only…

The phone vibrated in her palm. Joe, she thought. Calling to give her whatever details he could about the task that had gotten him up so early. Instead her boss's name came up on the caller ID. Surprised and just a little alarmed by the early call, Callie switched instantly from silent to speaker mode.

"Hi, Simona. Is everything okay?"

"No! Everything is *not* okay." Anger, hot and scorching, jumped through the speaker. "I want you at the center in fifteen minutes."

"Why? What's...?"

"Fifteen minutes! Not one minute later. *Capisce?*"

Agitation had stirred the director's accent. It was so thick and heavy Callie struggled to separate the furious words.

"If you take longer," her boss fumed. "If you are not here then, do not bother to come in. Just pack your bags. Go home!"

"Simona! Wait! Tell me—"

Too late. She was talking to dead air. Callie wasted several precious seconds debating whether to call her boss back. It wouldn't do any good, she realized. She needed a face-to-face to sort out whatever had Simona in such a fury. Tossing her phone aside, Callie raced for the bathroom.

She was out the door nine minutes later. Her duster flapped around her ankles as she hurried through streets just coming alive with morning traffic. With each step, she tried to figure out what she'd done to infuriate her boss.

Maybe it was her unconventional hair therapy. Had that backfired? Had one of the teens suffered a traumatic loss of identity after hacking off their long, beaded braids? Or Leela? Was the mutilated wife now mourning the loss of her hair? Could she feel it added to her disfigurement? Think that not even surgery would help her now?

Or was it Amal? Dear God, had she pushed Amal

too hard? Dragged the agreement to visit the Borghese out of her? Precipitated a panic attack? Her stomach clenching, Callie could visualize the pregnant woman springing out of bed, grabbing her pencil and viciously slashing another drawing.

With her thoughts roiling, she rounded the corner and blew out a relieved breath. Whatever had precipitated the director's summons apparently hadn't included a call to outside authorities. No police cars, no fire trucks, no ambulances or flashing strobes of any kind were parked in front of the center. The terra cotta building sat dark and silent, showing only the dim outline of a single lighted window on the ground floor.

Her office. That was her office.

More confused now than apprehensive, Callie slapped her palm against the keypad and yanked the door open. She started down the dimly lit hallway but had taken only a few steps when she caught the back-and-forth of angry voices coming from her office.

Simona. And Carlo. Trading such fast and furious Italian that Callie couldn't catch even a gist of their heated conversation. She was about to call out when something banged against the metal file cabinet and Simona issued what sounded like a sneering taunt. Then, suddenly, the taunt ended on a squawk.

Uh-oh. This was not good. Not good at all.

Like a bright red warning light, the prince's startling revelation that he itched to kiss the condescending smirk off the director's face flashed in Callie's head. She almost turned tail and ran. A sharp crack and a growled curse held her in place. Her imagination running riot, she decided she'd better make her presence known. Like now.

"Simona? Carlo?"

She heard a rattle. A thump that sounded like the legs of her office chair hitting the floor. Her boss's angry acknowledgment.

"In your office!"

The tableau that greeted her confirmed her worst fears. Simona bristled with fury and Carlo's cheek sported a fat red blotch.

"You, uh, wanted to see me?"

"No." Simona's arm whipped out. A rigid index finger stabbed at the flickering screen of Callie's desktop. "I wanted you to see this."

"Why did you boot up my computer?" Callie asked in confusion. "Did yours crash?"

"*I* didn't boot it up. It was on when I got here."

Thoroughly confused, Callie looked from her to Carlo and back again. "Who turned it on, then? Nikki? One of the mental-health techs?"

The prince rubbed his cheek and took it from there. Shooting an angry glance at his nemesis, he answered stiffly.

"None of the other staff members have come in yet. *Il Drago* found the computer on when she arrived. At which point she called me and started ranting about my having another judge on my payroll. One who would authorize access to your case files."

A chill slithered down Callie's spine. "Someone… someone got into my case files?"

"So it appears," Simona threw at her. "Unless you forgot to log out and shut your computer down last night."

"Of course I logged out!"

Carlo aimed another glance at the director and tried to soften what was feeling more and more like an inquisition. "Are you certain, Callie?"

"Yes!"

Or...

Frantically, she searched her memory. Images flashed by like a slide show. She'd talked to Amal. Confirmed the tickets for the Borghese. Gone down to her office. Logged on and updated the case file. Logged out and hurried to brief Simona on the breakthrough.

Another series of images popped into her head. Of Joe helping Emilio scan the staff and residents' palm prints into the new electronic key pads. One after another. With plenty of time in between to take a break. Amble down the hall. Scope out Callie's office.

No! She wouldn't go there! She couldn't!

Despite the fierce self-denial, a sick feeling curled in the pit of her stomach. She'd jotted down the password, she now remembered. Aleppo221. She'd reversed the digits but acknowledged now that wasn't much of a challenge for a determined hacker.

Her office was too small and crowded to get to her desk. The sick feeling spread from her stomach to her lungs as she uttered a bleak request. "Simona, look under the blotter."

"Why?"

"Just do it."

The director took two steps and jerked up the blotter. The violent movement dislodged the sticky. It floated free and drifted down to lie on the desktop like an accusing yellow eye.

"You wrote down the pass code?" Simona breathed fire. "And left it where any *idiota* might find it?"

Callie couldn't answer. Couldn't breathe. But she could visualize the yesterday's scene as if it replayed in high definition.

Joe and her. Standing toe to toe in this same office.

Not every resident's home of origin was documented, she'd informed him. And even if was, the case file containing that information was protected. She couldn't disclose it without the written consent of the individuals involved. And she could hear his answer. As terse and sharp as a hammer striking iron.

So get their consent.

She staggered back a step as another scene spun through in her mind, too vivid to block. Joe and Emilio. So clever. So skilled. Circumventing legal requirements by plugging an absurdly long override code into the keypads at the center's front and back entrances. Then waiting in the hall when Callie dashed upstairs to tell Amal she'd booked museum tickets.

No! Joe wouldn't search her desk. He wouldn't hack into her files.

Would he?

Stabbed through the heart by sudden, crippling uncertainty, Callie spun on her heel. She ignored the director's sharp command to come back. Ignored Carlo's urgent plea to talk this through. She wanted no part of either of them. No part of the pain that clawed at her heart.

Joe was bent over a map of Rome when his phone buzzed. A quick glance at caller ID showed Carlo's photo and phone number. He hit Connect, knowing his friend's face would flash up on the other end.

"Yeah?"

"We need you at the center," the prince barked. "Now!"

His pulse kicked. "Why?"

"Simona. She called me. Callie, too."

"Callie's there?"

"She was. She just stormed out."

"On my way."

* * *

Callie wandered aimlessly. She didn't notice the city springing to life around her, had no idea where she was. She couldn't focus enough to identify any landmarks.

Her thoughts centered on Joe. Only Joe.

He'd promised, she thought, her heart twisting. That morning in Naples. Before they'd explored Pompeii. He hadn't liked being pinned to the mat. Still, he'd agreed that theirs had to be a marriage of equals. Reluctantly, she remembered, and only after grabbing the out she'd offered him with both hands.

Extraordinary circumstances. That was the out. Had he used it? Made a unilateral decision to access the files?

Blind to the traffic beginning to churn the streets, Callie turned a corner. Two seconds later she stopped dead. Oh, sweet Jesus! Not the fountain! Not now, with the silly, *stupid* wish she'd made three months ago rising up to mock her.

She turned away. Made it several yards down one of the three streets leading away from the fountain before she surrendered to its inexorable pull. Her feet dragging, she turned and retraced her steps.

Thankfully, it was too early for the usual horde of tourists. Only a hardy few had braved the cold to add their contribution to the more than three thousand euros tossed in the fountain's basin every year. The offerings of these early risers hit with dull thunks. Callie saw why when she threaded through the sparse crowd.

How appropriate! How ironically appropriate! Rome's iconic fountain was bone dry.

With a hiccuping laugh, she sank onto the steps leading down to the basin. Last night she'd wandered Rome's beautifully illuminated streets and marveled at how magical the city was at Christmas. Now it felt as cold and empty as the fountain and too dreary for words.

Yet... Dammit! She hated to tuck tail and scurry home like a scolded child. Yes, she'd screwed up. Yes, she'd left a barely disguised version of her computer's password where person or persons unknown might find it. But every time she tried to pin Joe's face on that nebulous someone, her heart stuttered.

Shoulders hunched, nose sniffling in the cold, Callie burrowed her chin in her coat collar and stared unseeing at Oceanus and his pawing steeds. Joe hadn't violated her trust. He wouldn't. The certainty seeped into her heart slowly. Steadily. Replacing the doubt with a soul-deep relief.

She had no idea how long she'd been sitting there, lost in thought, when an excited exclamation pierced the cold morning air.

"Oh! Look!"

Callie's glance cut from the wide-eyed coed just a few feet away to the fountain. It came alive right before her eyes. Water trickled into the top basin. The sun had arced high enough now to add a frosty sparkle as the stream filled that marble bowl.

"They've turned on the fountain." The young coed a few feet away threw Callie an excited grin. "Isn't that awesome?"

"Totally."

The trickle gained volume. The top basin spilled into the second. Its overflow emptied into the third. That overflow fanned sideways. Soon the splash into a half dozen marble shells filled the air. Breathlessly, Callie watched as the giant circular basin at the fountain's base began to fill.

* * *

Joe didn't need a GPS lock to know exactly where to look for her. Sure enough, he spotted her huddled against the cold and sitting shoulder to shoulder with a young woman sporting a Stanford University backpack. The two of them were completely absorbed in the spectacle of the Trevi Fountain coming to life.

He hung back, remembering the last time they'd gathered at this same fountain. Him, Carlo, Travis and Kate, Dawn and Brian and Tommy. And Callie, of the pansy eyes and serene smile. He still found it incredible that none of her friends had seen the worry she'd hidden behind that Mona Lisa facade. Even more incredible that he'd pierced her stubborn defense and gotten her to trust him.

That trust now hung by a thread. After Carlo's terse account of the confrontation at the center, Joe knew she had to think he'd betrayed her. Rehearsing and discarding a dozen different approaches, he settled for simply saying her name.

Her hips swiveled. Her head turned. Those soul-stripping eyes locked with his. "Hello, Joe. Tugging on my electronic leash?"

"We need to talk."

She gave a short laugh. "I thought that was my line."

The coed flashed an uncertain look from her to Joe and back again. "Do you want me to hang with you awhile?" she asked Callie.

"No. But thanks for the offer."

"You sure?"

"I'm sure. Go ahead, make a wish."

The twentysomething pushed to her feet, all long-legged grace and unfettered energy. She tipped her backpack off one shoulder and rooted around in its cavernous depth for several moments.

Joe preempted her and produced a coin. "Here."

She hesitated and threw another glance at Callie. At her nod, the college student accepted the euro with a mumbled, "Thanks."

Joe sank down in the spot she'd just vacated. Hip to hip, he and Callie watched the young woman face away from the fountain. The euro sailed in a clean arc over her shoulder and splashed into the half-full basin. She turned, spotted the ripples, and gave a jaunty thumbs-up before joining several others her own age for a flurry of group shots and selfies.

"I hope she gets her wish," Callie murmured.

Joe didn't answer for the simple reason that he didn't think a reply was required. Beside him, Callie drew up her knees and rested her chin on the flap of her coat.

"Do you remember the last time we were here?" she asked after a moment, her gaze on the glistening water.

"I remember."

"We made a wish then, Dawn and Kate and I. Should I tell you what my wish was?"

Joe wasn't sure he wanted to know. When he made a noncommittal sound, she angled her chin and pinned him with those incredible eyes.

"I wished for a dreamy romantic hero, *à la* Louis Jourdan," she confessed.

"Who?"

"He was one of the stars in the original movie version *Three Coins in the Fountain*."

Right. Nothing like losing out to some '50s-era matinee idol he'd never heard of.

"A dreamy romantic hero, huh? Sorry, sweetheart. Looks like you scored zero for three."

"Actually," she countered, "I think I scored three for three."

He was still digesting that when she scooted around on the step so they were knee to knee. Pulling off her glove, she feathered her fingertips across his cheek.

"I don't want movie star flash and dash, Joe. I want a real hero. One who's earned his stripes the hard way. One who would never lie to me or betray my trust."

He captured her hand and held it against his cheek. "I didn't hack into those files, Callie."

"I know."

"Nor did any of my crew."

"I know." Her mouth twisted in a grimace. "I admit I freaked when Simona confronted me this morning. It was such a shock, coming out of the blue like that. But once I got here, once I took time to think things through, I knew you wouldn't renege on our agreement."

Joe wanted to let this moment spin out. Given a choice, he would've kept the ugliness at bay until their butts froze to the cold marble step. Unfortunately, he didn't have that option. He needed to bring Callie up to speed and get them both back to the center.

"We've verified the breach didn't originate in-house," he told her. "The hacker overrode the password and powered up your computer from a remote device."

"Device?" She glanced quickly from side to side and lowered her voice. "Like a laptop?"

"Yeah."

She took a moment to process that. "You said he overrode the password. So he didn't use the one I scribbled on a note and stuck to the underside of my blotter?"

"No, but remind me to teach you some of the finer points of computer security."

"Oh, Joe! I'm so glad. Well, not *glad*. But I thought…

Simona and I both thought…" She blew out a frosty breath. "Well, let's just say I was getting ready to pack my bags."

Joe could have relieved everyone's mind about that a lot sooner if he'd instructed Emilio to activate the interior cameras he'd installed yesterday. The hidden eyes would've picked up anyone entering or exiting Callie's office.

Well, that hurdle was now cleared. According to Carlo's terse account, he'd informed an outraged Simona that the cameras were in place and were going active until further notice. Di Lorenzo hadn't related her response.

"Have you determined the location of this remote device?" Callie wanted to know.

"Not yet. But we're close."

They damned well should be, with cybergeeks on two continents pulling out all the stops. Joe's people, DIA, NSA, their Italian counterparts, even Brian Ellis, whose skunkworks cadre sat elbow to elbow with the members of the Military Satellite Communications Systems division at Los Angeles Air Force Station.

"We're also close to tagging which files he went into, if any," Joe told her. "Once we have that information, we can talk to the subjects. And hopefully nail down who's so interested in them, and why."

"That's skirting pretty close to the line," Callie worried. "Simona might object."

"Carlo can take that one on. From what he's told me, he and Simona have been duking it out all morning."

"Um. Not quite *all* morning."

Joe cocked his head. "You know something I don't?"

"Maybe. When we get back to the center, you might want to ask Carlo if his cheek still stings."

"Huh?"

"Just ask him. In the meantime…" She got up and brushed off the seat of her coat. "I guess we should head back. I'd like to find out if I still have a job."

"Hold on." Joe unfolded his tall frame. "You say you got your wish. I sure don't see myself as dreamy or romantic or much of a hero, but what the hell. As long as it works for you."

"It works. Believe me, Joe, it works."

"Maybe. But this is what works for me."

Her nose was cold, her lips almost as chilled. They warmed under his, though, and sent a welcome heat rolling through his veins. When he raised his head, the smile in her eyes confirmed that all was right between them.

"Since that seems to have worked out so well," she said, "maybe I should make another wish."

"Sure you want to tempt fate twice?"

"Pretty sure. Do you have another euro?"

He watched as she took the coin and assumed the proper position with her back to the fountain. Eyes closed, she looked as though she was sorting through dozens of possibilities before settling on one. Then she sent the coin sailing to join the others in the basin.

"You going to tell me what you wished for this time, too?"

"Only after it comes true," she laughed.

Joe still had the specter of a supposedly dead terrorist hanging over him. Still had a hinky feeling in his gut that things were about to break. Yet that laugh made him feel a thousand pounds lighter.

The feeling lasted for all of five minutes. Just until he and Callie were weaving through the jumble of tourist stalls beginning to open for business on the Via Delle

Mutate. They were still several blocks from the center when Joe's phone buzzed. One glance at caller ID had him whipping up the phone.

"Russo."

"He's there." Frank Harden's voice stabbed through the instrument. "In Rome."

Chapter Thirteen

With Harden's warning ringing in his head, Joe hit speed dial and called for another war council at the center ASAP. By the time he and Callie got there, Emilio and Dominic were on their way. Carlo hadn't left the center yet. They found him pacing the hall, nursing a cup of coffee and a fierce scowl.

"Where's Simona?" Callie asked. "I need to know if I still have a job."

"Upstairs. One of the residents is ill."

"Oh, no! Is Nikki with her?"

"Not yet. Dominic just texted. She's coming in with him."

"I'd better go up and see if I can help."

She shed her coat and scarf, tossed them in her office, and hurried up the stairs.

That left Joe to relay Harden's terse message. When he had, Carlo cursed and tossed his half-empty cup in a trash can.

"It's not yet eight o'clock and the morning has already become a nightmare. First *il Drago* wakes me from a very pleasant and most interesting dream. Then she drags me down here, only to fling accusations at me about bribing half the judges in Rome. And then, when I try to deny the absurd charge, she snorts and says I probably wouldn't remember who I've bribed, anyway."

Having worked the prince's security for several months, Joe would bet his last dollar that Carlo was more riled over the forgetfulness charge than the bribery. Sure enough, the prince tugged at one end of his mustache and sputtered indignantly.

"She all but called me senile. Me!"

Callie's earlier remark teased at Joe's brain. He wanted to ignore it. And he didn't want to hear any further details in what could turn out to be a very awkward situation. But Carlo's outrage demanded a response.

"So you, uh, offered to prove that you're still young and virile?"

"What? But no! I merely kissed her."

Joe tried, he really tried, to block the image of Carlo laying one on Simona Alberti.

"So," he said when the image wouldn't go away, "she whacked you a good one."

"A *very* good one." His outrage subsiding, Carlo slipped into a rueful grin and rubbed his cheek. "I should recruit her for the Stormo Incursori, no? My commandos could use someone who packs as much firepower in one arm as that one does."

"Better we brief her on Frank Harden's call," Joe suggested, pulling the prince back to the present. "She needs to know whoever hacked into the case files is here, in Rome."

Carlo nodded, but any plans to make the director

aware of the threat took a sharp U-turn when Callie flew halfway down the stairs. Her eyes wide under her cap of curls, she leaned so far over the wrought-iron rail that Joe almost shouted a warning.

"Amal's in labor," she announced excitedly, "and Simona says the baby's crowning! I've already called nine-one-one. We need scissors or a sharp knife and some string."

She whirled and flew back up the stairs, leaving the two men to exchange looks of sheer male panic.

"Do you know anything about delivering a baby?" Carlo asked with a touch of desperation.

"Only what's in the special ops medical handbook. You?"

"The same."

Swallowing a groan, Joe took off at a lope. "I'll hit the kitchen. They'll have a knife. Maybe some string. You check the offices."

Like Carlo, Joe had spent years in clandestine ops. More years prior to that as a military cop. During those years, he'd put his emergency medical training to the test more times than he wanted to count. Most recently, he remembered like a bayonet to the heart, in Curaçao. Cursing, he shoved that bloody scene out of his head. This was here. This was now.

As he raced for the kitchen, he dredged up a mental image of the special ops medical handbook. There was a chapter on obstetrics, he remembered. Not anywhere as detailed as the chapters dealing with treating battle-field injuries, of course. But pretty damned thorough. The subheadings faded in, faded out, jumped into focus.

Stage One: Onset of cervical changes and uterine contractions.

Stage Two: Full dilation and birth.

Stage Three: Delivery of the placenta.

Okay. Okay. Callie said the baby was crowing. That meant Amal had already progressed to stage two.

Images from the memorized manual flashed into Joe's head. Diagrams of the female reproductive organs. Other diagrams showing a fully formed baby in the birth canal. Instructions on assisting a breech birth. How to do a...

What the hell was that incision? Damned if he could remember the medical term for a cut might be necessary to keep the baby from tearing the vaginal wall and ripping into the rectum, causing a bacterial infection that could kill both mother and child.

Christ Almighty!

He slammed into the kitchen and scared the crap out of the two cooks preparing what smelled like spicy breakfast frittatas. Good thing they recognized Joe from his survey of ingress and egress routes or he might have been smacked in the face with a giant frying pan. Still, they tensed and looked ready to let fly when he grabbed a long knife from the preparation counter.

"The director... Signora Alberti...she needs this." Whirling, he plunged the blade into a pot of boiling water. "And string. *Corda.* Do you have *corda*?"

One of the cooks pointed his spatula at a drawer in the counter. Joe pawed through the jumble and found a roll of plastic twine. He was out of the kitchen and halfway to the stairs when he remembered Emilio. Juggling the knife and twine, he got his phone out of his pocket and stabbed a speed-dial number.

"Where the hell are you?"

"I'm just parking."

"You have your med kit with you?"

"In the dash. Why?"

"It's got sterile gloves, right? Gauze? And scissors. We need scissors."

"*Mio Dio!* What's happened?"

"A baby. That's what's happening."

"Amal? Is it Amal?"

"Yeah! Now get your ass in here!"

Callie's only experience with live birth had occurred when she was nine or ten years old. One otherwise uneventful Thursday evening, the gray-and-white cat who'd adopted her some years previously had mewled and pawed a nest in Callie's fluffy pink bedspread. With no further ado, Boots proceeded to deliver seven adorable kittens.

This birth looked to be considerably more nerve-racking for everyone involved. A panting, white-faced Amal half sat, half reclined in her favorite chair in the arts and crafts room. Hidden behind the artificial palm draped with handmade stars and silver tinsel, she'd obviously been sketching when her pains first stabbed into her. Her pencil and a head and shoulders crafted with her signature bold strokes lay at the side of the chair, kicked out of the way by Simona and Leela.

The director now knelt between Amal's knees. The center's emergency medical kit and a stack of folded white towels were close at hand. Leela crouched beside the straining woman, gripping her hand and murmuring encouragement in her precise English. Another woman, one whose name Callie couldn't remember, stood on Amal's other side and dabbed her sweat-streaked face with a cool cloth.

Other residents crowded the hall and corners of the large room. As Callie hurried past them, she thought for a heart-wrenching moment that she could tell those who'd had—and lost—children by the mix of hope and desolation on their faces. Aching for them, she issued a breathless report.

"Scissors and some string are on the way, Simona."

"Good, because this little one's about to make his or her debut." The director was calm, cool, rock steady. "Push now, Amal. Push. Once more. Ah, there he is. I'm holding his head. One more… Wait. Wait!"

She flashed a look over her shoulder and caught Callie in a relentless stare. "Grab one of those towels. Now kneel beside me and support the baby's head. No, don't elevate it. Just hold it steady."

Still calm, still steady, the director explained what she was doing to the panting mother. "The umbilical cord is wrapped around your baby's neck. That's not uncommon. My second baby came the same way."

Callie barely registered the words. Her entire being was concentrated on the folded towel that cradled the tiny head crowned with wet, matted black hair.

"There," Simona said. "I'm loosening the cord, making the loop bigger. Now the shoulders can slip through. All right. Push."

When the baby slid into Simona's hands, none of the women in the room uttered a single sound. The incredible drama gripped Callie, too. She could hardly breathe as Simona gently turned the baby over and cleared its mouth with a gloved finger. Then the baby's lusty wail broke the spell. Relief and excitement pulsed through the room in palpable waves.

"It's a girl." The director's voice wavered for the briefest instant as she wrapped the baby in a clean towel and placed the bundle in Amal's outstretched arms. "A beautiful little girl."

Joe heard the pronouncement as he angled his way

through the crowd at the door. Carlo was right behind him, and he could hear Emilio thundering up the stairs. He wanted to believe their services weren't needed but knew they weren't in the clear yet. Someone still had to cut the cord…and take care of the afterbirth. He was hoping to hell he could pass the knife and twine to someone more qualified to perform those tasks when he caught the wail of a siren. It was followed almost instantly by Carlo's fervent prayer of thanks.

"Grazie a Dio!"

Nikki arrived on the scene the same time as the EMTs. Only too happy to yield her place to professionals, Callie pushed to her feet. As she edged around the potted palm, she spotted Amal's discarded sketch. She swooped it up to keep it from being trampled by the medical team but was too absorbed in the continuing drama to give the portrait more than a passing glance.

She was still holding it when the EMTs transferred Amal and her baby to a gurney and wheeled them out. Nikki went with them, leaving Simona to share warm hugs with Leela and the woman who'd mopped Amal's sweaty face. She hugged Callie, too, in a rare moment of pure sentiment.

As the crowd of residents slowly dispersed, Simona went into a bathroom to wash off the blood and fluids. When she came downstairs some time later, she was wearing a borrowed skirt so long it dragged the floor and a T-shirt obviously donated by the younger of the two teens. A female rock star Callie didn't recognize flashed a dazzlingly white smile across Simona's breasts.

"Good, you're still here."

She crossed to Callie, standing in the hall with Joe, Carlo, Emilio and Nikki's husband, Dominic.

"I'm sorry I railed at you earlier about the password. After you ran out, Joe told us someone hacked the case files via a remote device."

"No," Callie protested. "You were right to be angry. It was stupid of me to write the password down."

"Well, that's water under the bridge."

"It is?" Carlo asked, feigning amazement. "Am I hearing right? Is *il Drago* tempering her fire?"

"Not when it matters," Simona warned.

"Ah. Then I must assume you won't apologize to me."

"You assume right," Simona huffed. "You deserved to have your face slapped."

"I was not speaking of that." The mocking gleam in his eyes softened. "But since you mention it, *cara*, I must tell you it was worth the pain."

To the surprise and acute discomfort of their audience, a tide of red crawled up Simona's creased cheeks. She countered it with a reply that dripped unadulterated acid.

"Then what *were* you speaking of?"

"Hmm. Let me think." Carlo pretended confusion this time. "I'm trying to remember."

He glanced from Joe to Emilio to Dominic, his expression comical.

"*Santa Maria!* I must be growing senile." He turned a helpless look on Simona. "Did you…? Did you…? Help me, *cara*! Did you accuse me of having judges in my pocket?"

Her reply was a glacial stare.

Callie caught her breath as the light of battle leaped

into the prince's face. Thank God Joe intervened before blood was spilled.

"Why don't we take this to your office, Simona? I need to tell you about the call I got earlier this morning while Callie and I were on our way back to the center. I briefed her and Carlo, but you and Emilio and Dominic need to know the latest."

The director glared at him, obviously reluctant to surrender the field. But concern for her charges won out over her private war with the prince. Hitching up her ridiculously long skirt, she headed for her office.

Carlo didn't try to disguise his disappointment at her capitulation. Joe, Dominic and Emilio, however, shared a glance of profound relief. Callie ignored all four as the director's calm, steady assurances to Amal echoed in her mind.

That's not uncommon.

My second baby came the same way.

She let the others go on ahead. Simona's words kept ringing in her head.

Callie was a trained psychologist. She'd studied at two of the most reputable universities in the United States. If her ego had needed stroking, she could've hung her framed diplomas in her office. Yet every day, every client reinforced how rarely life conformed to textbook case studies.

Simona's past was obviously as complex and tortured as Joe's, yet they'd both defied the odds. Somehow, some way, they'd drawn on inner reserves to emerge stronger and more resilient than anyone would've predicted.

And Amal, or whatever her real name was. She'd given birth surrounded by strangers. No screams. No tears. Only muffled grunts as she delivered the child she must pray would grow up in a safe, stable world.

Humbled again by Amal's courage, Callie glanced at the portrait she'd scooped off the floor. She'd almost forgotten she held it and swore softly when she saw her nervous fist had crunched the paper. Carefully, she smoothed the folds.

As before, Amal's talent astounded her. The bold, confident strokes. The clean lines. The pride and...

Wait! She knew that face! But how? Where?

She made the connection just seconds later. Amal had sketched the same face a few days ago. So arrogant. So beautiful. Then she'd slashed the sketch, over and over and over, until she'd obliterated it.

Callie had thought then—she *still* thought—the drawing represented some unidentified, unspecified male figure from Amal's past. A masculine amalgam that summarized her deep-seated hate and fear.

Yet the longer Callie stared at this portrait, the more convinced she became it wasn't an abstract rendering. This man had lived and breathed. His face was so real and alive and...

Oh, God! She'd seen him! Just the other morning! She'd spilled white chocolate espresso on his sleeve, then earned a fierce glare when she'd asked if the foam had seeped into his computer. His *laptop* computer.

Barely able to breathe, Callie gripped the sketch in suddenly icy hands. Could this man be the target? The one who'd escaped the drone strike? Had he made those online queries about the center? And hacked into the case files? The possibilities were too real and too frightening to ignore.

Her heart thumping, she hurried down the hall. A few yards from the director's office, she abruptly stopped.

She could hear the conversation inside. Joe. Simona. Joe again. Their low voices competed with the warnings now firing through her mind.

Amal had sketched this portrait here, at the center. A place that promised her sanctuary and every expectation of privacy. Was this drawing covered by client-counselor privilege? Would Callie violate that privilege if she showed it to outsiders?

As soon as the thought occurred, she killed it. If the man in this sketch was who Joe thought he might be, he represented a potential danger to Amal. Possibly everyone at the center. Callie would take full responsibility for showing the portrait to appropriate authorities.

She pushed through the door and thrust the crumpled sketch at Joe. "Amal drew this. I don't know who the man is, but I've seen him. Just a few days ago. At the café around the corner. He was having espresso... and he had a laptop with him."

The others crowded around to study the portrait.

"Anyone recognize him?" Joe asked.

When no one did, he whipped out his phone and snapped several quick shots.

"I'm forwarding these to Harden and my own people," he said, his thumbs working. "To you, too, Carlo, so you can send them to your contacts in the *polizia*. Emilio, I want you to zap a copy to every man on your crew. Have them canvass the neighborhood. Start with the café where Callie spotted this guy. And get someone to the hospital. I want a watch on Amal's room 24/7."

"Do you think she's in danger?" Simona asked sharply. "Her and the baby?"

"I don't know. Let's hope to hell she can answer that. You'd better come with me. You and Callie."

"It might be better if Emilio talks to her," Callie suggested.

Joe's glance sawed into her. "You think I might frighten her?"

The scar. He thought she was worried about the scar. Her chin lifting, she met that absurdity head-on.

"You have to admit you can be pretty intimidating when you want to," she replied calmly. "But I was thinking of yesterday morning. Emilio actually got Amal to talk to him. And she told me that she thought he had a kind face."

Joe snorted, and the others all turned to study the face under discussion. It immediately turned brick red. Thoroughly embarrassed, Emilio said gruffly that he'd be happy to accompany them to the hospital.

The Ospedale San Giovanni Addolorata was a massive complex in the heart of Rome, located right behind the Egyptian obelisk and within sight of the Colosseum. Interactive displays in the hospital's main entrance depicted its long history, while plexiglass cutouts in the tiled floor gave glimpses the long-buried ruins of the home of Emperor Marcus Aurelius's mother.

A call to Nikki confirmed that Amal and the baby had already been transferred from the ER to the maternity ward. Getting to the ward proved quite a challenge. Signs directed Callie and the others to another building, then to two different banks of elevators and, finally, to the wing containing the obstetrical delivery suites, nursery and neonatal intensive care unit. Their small group drew several glances along the way. Particularly Simona in her gaudy borrowed T-shirt, dragging skirt and flyaway dandelion hair. Blithely ignoring the stares, she marched up to the nurses' station where Nikki was filling out forms.

"How are they?"

"Fine. The doctor has examined them both. The baby's in the nursery, and Amal's getting cleaned up a bit. I'll need some help with this paperwork." Nikki made a helpless gesture at the forms. "She still won't give us her name or any other identifying information."

"I'll talk to her. What room is she in?"

"Three twelve. Second door on the left."

When the director headed for the room, Nikki gave Callie a quick smile. "You did well this morning."

"I didn't do anything. Amal and Simona did all the work."

"Well, the result was worth their effort. The baby's beautiful."

"You said she's in the nursery?"

"She is. There's a viewing window just there, down the hall."

Nikki went back to her paperwork, Emilio went in search of coffee and Callie waited for Joe to finish checking his text messages.

"I wanted to make sure my contacts received the sketch," he told her when he finished. "They have, and they're running facial recognition programs. If he's in the system, we'll ID him."

"I'm going to see the baby. Want to come with me?"

"Sure."

The shades were up, giving an unimpeded view of the plastic bassinets in their stainless steel stands. Most were empty. The babies were probably with their moms, Callie guessed, being nursed or bathed or cuddled. Only three bassinets were occupied.

In one, the baby wore a blue stocking cap. The other

two wore pink. Both still had the scrunched-up red faces of newborns, but the baby on the left had to be Amal's. The silky black hair peeking below her stocking cap was a dead giveaway. That, and the name on the bassinet. Callie had to squint to make out the hand lettering. When she did, she caught her breath.

Simona. Amal had named her baby Simona.

The rightness of it put a smile around Callie's heart. She hoped it would put one around the director's, too.

"Which one is Amal's?" Joe asked.

"The one on the left."

"How can you tell?"

"Look at the name on the bassinet."

Like Callie, he had to squint. Unlike her, though, he wasn't as confident about the rightness of it.

"I don't know much about your boss's past," he said quietly. "Carlo doesn't, either. Only that she was married once and lost her family in some kind of natural disaster. Hard to imagine how someone who's lost so much will feel about having a namesake."

"I think she'll love it," Callie murmured. Her gaze lingered on the pink stocking cap and tufts of black hair. "Cradling that little head in my hands this morning at the moment of her birth was the most amazing thing I've ever experienced."

With a last glance at the baby, she angled away from the window.

"We haven't talked about having kids, Joe. How do you feel about having a namesake?"

"Just say the word." One of his rare smiles tipped his mouth. "Kate and Dawn would probably advise you to take a trip down the aisle first, but I'm ready any time you are."

"I'm ready, too. For both."

It took a moment for that to register. When it did, his smile became a full-fledged grin. "How does a Christmas wedding sound?"

"Oh, I would love that! But I can't fly home, even for a few days, and leave Simona in the lurch."

"So we have the wedding here."

"But..."

"Kate and Dawn. Yeah, I know. Reminds me of that old saying."

Callie arched a brow.

"If a frog had wheels, it wouldn't bump its butt."

Her other brow rose. "What does that mean?"

"Damned if I know. Gran says it all the time, though." Curling a knuckle under her chin, he tipped her face to his. "Let me work the details, Pansy Eyes. All you'll have to do is—"

"Joe! Callie!" Nikki waved to them. "Simona wants us to join her in Amal's room."

Chapter Fourteen

"He is my husband's brother."

Amal didn't look at them. Gripping the hospital blanket with white-knuckled fists, she stared at wall above their heads.

"He was to drive the car. The one that was hit. But he suspected someone had betrayed him. Coward that he is, he sent his brother to die in his place."

She dropped her gaze, glaring at them as her words gained heat and fury.

"My husband was not like him! He was gentle and kind and would have nothing to do with his brother's hate-filled friends! That's why they tricked him into driving the car. Why he followed at a safe distance, sending messages on his computer to others in their cadre, waiting to see if my husband sprang the trap they'd suspected."

Her fists convulsed on the blanket. Her face, her eyes, her body language all conveyed rage.

"He would kill me, too. I knew what he had done. He could not let me live to tell of his shameful cowardice. So I fled. And when the boat sank and I swam ashore, I told no one my name. Told no one where I'd come from."

She stopped, breathing hard and fast as the memories tore at her. Then her fire shaded to fear.

"I thought we were safe, my baby and I. Now Simona says… She says he may be here. In Rome. Is that true?"

Joe didn't pad the truth. "We think so."

"You must find him! Please! Before he finds me and my baby."

"We plan to. Until we do, Emilio will stand guard. He and the *polizia*. They'll protect you and the baby."

"I'm staying, too," Simona announced. "Callie, you'll go with Joe back to the center, won't you?"

"Of course."

"Explain what's happened to the staff and other residents. Show them the sketch and tell them to be especially aware when they go out."

They were in the SUV, just pulling up at the center, when Joe got a call from Carlo. He screeched the vehicle to a halt with a terse explanation.

"One of Emilio's crew spotted him. He's having espresso at the same little café where you bumped into him. The *polizia* are on their way. Wait here at the center."

She knew better than to suggest she should go with him. Joe didn't need to be worrying about keeping her safe. She wanted him to focus on keeping himself safe! Her heart banged against her ribs as he shouldered the door open.

"Be careful!"

"I will."

He tore off the moment she hit the keypad and was safely inside. The café was just around the corner. She would hear the sirens when the police arrived. Only if they hit the sirens, she amended. They might not want to alert him.

She had no idea how long she stayed rooted just inside the door. Her hands shoved in her pockets, she repeated again and again the wish she'd made just a few hours ago at the Trevi Fountain.

And then it was over.

No flash, no bang, no police sirens.

Just Joe pulling up in the black SUV to deliver another quick report. Callie spotted the monster vehicle through a front window and ran outside almost before he'd braked to a halt. The driver's side window whirred down, and Callie hung on the door while he shared the news.

"We got him. Bastard was too busy banging away on his laptop to realize we had him in our sights. He tried to run when the *polizia* arrived." His mouth tipped in a wolfish grin. "Didn't get far."

"Are you sure it's him? Amal's brother-in-law?"

"Almost one hundred percent. Carlo's going to the hospital with one of the police officers. They'll nail down the last one percent."

"Thank God!"

"I'm heading downtown to share what I know with the anti-terror unit." He put the SUV in gear but kept his foot on the brake. "When I get back, we need to finish the discussion we were having at the hospital. The one about namesakes and Christmas weddings."

Callie was so overjoyed that the worry and fear might

finally be over that she would have married him right there, in the street. She settled for leaning through the window and hooking an arm around him to drag him down for a kiss.

"You take care of the bad guy. I'll take care of the wedding."

Naturally, her first call was to Kate and Dawn. She couldn't wait. Still standing in the street, she woke first one, then the other and had to assure both that she hadn't yanked them from sleep because she was hurt or had been in an accident or had dumped Joe.

"Just the opposite. We're getting married."

"When?" Dawn shrieked.

"Where?" Kate yelped.

"That depends on whether Brian's corporate jet's available in the next few days."

"To fly you home?"

"To fly you guys here. I know it's short notice and you've probably got family coming for Christmas. Brian's folks, or yours and Travis's, Kate. But if you can make it, I would—"

"Don't be stupid. Of course we'll make it. Just tell us where you want us when."

"Christmas Eve. Here in Rome. I haven't worked all the details yet. I'll get back to you as soon as I do."

"What about your folks?" Dawn asked. "The jet has plenty of room if they want to come."

"Thanks for the offer. I doubt they'll want to fly over, but I'll call and check."

She gripped the phone, suddenly teary eyed with emotion and drippy nosed from the cold.

"This has been the most amazing morning," she sniffed. "I almost got fired and I helped deliver a baby.

Then Joe and Carlo took down a really, really nasty bad guy. Oh, and I tossed a coin in the Trevi Fountain. The wish is already coming true."

"All that in one morning?"

Kate sounded amazed, but Dawn zeroed in instantly on the most significant of those events.

"Hot damn! The fountain scores again."

Callie gave a watery laugh. "Okay, I'm standing on the sidewalk freezing my ass off. I've got to go inside and make a bunch more calls. I'll get back to you as soon as I firm up the arrangements. Ciao. And thank you!"

Before she could start working her growing mental list of to-dos, she had to brief Leela and Sabeen and the other residents on the visit to the hospital. They greeted the news that both mother and baby were doing fine with happy smiles.

"We will visit her," Leela declared. "And take gifts for the baby."

Callie left them making arrangements and hurried to her office to make her own. It was still too early to contact her folks, so she called Carlo, intending to just leave a voice mail asking him to call her when he could. He picked up halfway through her message.

"Oh, I'm sorry. Are you at the hospital?"

"We're still on the way. I just spoke with Joe. He tells me you're to be married. Congratulations, *mia bella*, although I can't understand why you would wish to tie yourself to such a lout when you could fly with me to—"

"Yes, yes, I know. Casablanca or Antibes or wherever. Why don't you take Simona? You know you want to."

"Ha! She would not consider it for a moment." He hesitated a beat, two. "Would she?"

"You won't know until you ask. In the meantime, I might need a favor."

"You have only to name it."

"I haven't checked yet what kind of license or permit we'll need to get married in Italy on Christmas Eve. If it turns out there's a bureaucratic tangle, do you think you could you get one of your judges to slice through it?"

"Certainly. And may I make a suggestion? My home here in the city boasts a very large salon. It would give me great pleasure if you and Joe would have the ceremony there. With a supper to follow, perhaps?"

Callie's initial thought had been to hold the ceremony here at the center. Having it at the prince's palazzo would make it a treat for the residents and so very, very special for both Joe and her.

"Oh, Carlo, thank you! That would be wonderful!"

"*Bene*! I'll take care of getting the judge to conduct the ceremony, too, if you wish. One of those many in my pay," he added drily.

"Yes, and thank you again!"

She disconnected feeling slightly dazed. In the space of ten short minutes, she'd nailed down the time, the place, the matrons of honor, the judge, the wedding supper. That left a dress…and a ring for Joe.

She knew exactly how to nail those down, too. Yanking open her desk drawer, she searched for the business card she'd brought back from Naples with her. Luckily, she got through to the buffalo ranch and reached the person she wanted on the first try.

"Ciao, Arianna. It's Callie."

"How good to hear from you. How are you enjoying Rome and your new job?"

"I love both."

"We must have lunch when I come up to Rome. Perhaps next week, yes? I still have a few presents to buy and haven't seen the lights of the Fendi building yet."

"That's why I'm calling. Joe and I strolled down Via Condotti the other night, but those boutiques are way out of my price range. I thought maybe you could recommend a shop where I could get a wedding ring for him and a dress for me."

"But yes! I frequent many excellent shops. When is the wedding?"

"Christmas Eve. I know it's short notice, and I'm sure you have plans to spend that evening with your family, but we would love if any or all of the Audi family could attend."

"But yes!" she exclaimed again. "And I will drive up tomorrow. It's Saturday and all the Christmas shoppers will be out, so we must start early. Can you meet me at Caffè Domiziano, in the Piazza Navona? Shall we say nine o'clock?"

"I'll be there!"

Unbelievably, every hastily contrived plan came off without a hitch.

With Arianna's enthusiastic assistance, Callie found the perfect dress and a simple gold band for Joe. Carlo sent his head chef to consult with her on the menu for the wedding supper and lined up a judge to perform the ceremony. After filling out reams of paper, she and Joe obtained a special license and arranged for a representative from the US consulate to act as a witness.

When Amal and the baby returned from the hospital, the refugee broke down in tears and shared her real identity. As Callie had suspected, Rasha Hadid was a highly regarded artist whose work was on exhibit in museums in Damascus and Cairo and Athens. And now that she no longer had to fear her brother-in-law, she could accept the position she'd been offered as an adjunct professor at the University of Thessaloniki. But first, she and the baby must attend the wedding of two to whom they owed so much.

As joyous as Rasha's return was, Callie's happiness brimmed over even more on Christmas Eve morning. She and Joe drove separate cars out to Ciampino Airport to pick up Kate and Dawn and their husbands. Joe wheeled the monster SUV. Callie drove a smaller and more manageable Fiat from Emilio's fleet. They parked at the terminal that handled executive jets and were waiting when the sleek Gulfstream with the Ellis Aeronautical Systems logo on its tail swooped in for a landing. To their delight, the first person to exit when the stairs were let down was Tommy. He raced over to them with his usual energy and promptly announced he wasn't worried about Santa finding him in Rome.

"Dad says his radar is better than the one on the Gulfstream even, 'n' he'll leave presents for Buster back at home. Doggy treats 'n' stuff. Grandma and Granddad are taking care of him. They're gonna make sure he doesn't eat poop. Dogs do that sometimes."

"Good to know," Joe said solemnly, then shook hands with Travis and Brian. "Thanks for making the trip on such short notice."

"No way we could miss seeing the last of the Inseparables bite the dust," Travis assured him. He nodded to the three women wrapped in a fierce group hug punctuated by sniffles and tears of joy. "How long has it been since they've seen each other? Three weeks?"

"Closer to two," Brian drawled.

When they finally untangled, Callie gave all four males a quick kiss before sweeping Dawn and Kate toward the Fiat. "Six o'clock. Carlo's palazzo. See you there."

"Yeah," Joe confirmed, "you will."

Callie steered through Rome's center with maximum concentration and minimal wrong turns. Kate and Dawn twisted to see the Fendi building as they zipped past. The decorations weren't as awesome in daylight as in the photo Callie had texted, but they both vowed to hit the high-end shopping street before they flew back to the States. Fifteen minutes later Callie squeezed into a parking spot and took them up to her apartment.

They oohed over the warm yellow walls and ahhed over the view of St. Peter's from the tiny balcony. Then they shed their coats and got down to the serious business of checking out the contents of the boxes sitting on the bed and the dress bag hanging on the closet door.

Chapter Fifteen

Callie couldn't have imagined a more stunning setting for a wedding than Carlo's palazzo. When she and Kate and Dawn emerged from the limo Joe had sent to pick them up, they had to fight to keep from gawking at the elegant facade and butler who'd been waiting for them. As tall and aristocratic as his employer was short and muscular, the tuxedoed majordomo bowed and ushered them inside.

He must have sent some silent signal to the prince. As Callie and Kate and Dawn were shedding their coats, Carlo descended a flight of marble stairs wide enough to drive a tractor up. Looking astonishingly royal in a dress uniform crossed by a red sash studded with glittering medals and decorations, he greeted Kate and Dawn with kisses to both hands and cheeks.

His greeting to the bride was no less extravagant. "Ah, Clarissa. You look so beautiful. Are you sure you—"

"Yes," she interrupted hastily, cutting him off before he could make yet another offer to whisk her off to parts unknown. "I'm sure."

But she had to repeat her suggestion of a few days ago. "Why don't you take Simona? You know you want to."

"I did ask her," he answered with a scowl. "Her reply still burns my ears."

Laughing, Callie stooped to drop a kiss on his cheek. "I know you. You're too much like Joe to take no for an answer."

"Perhaps. Perhaps not. But now…" He crooked his arm. "You break my heart, Clarissa, but do me such great honor by asking me to give you away. Shall we go upstairs?"

Her friends led the way. Dawn had brought a gown in her favorite green. Kate wore one of deep crimson. The rich hues formed a glowing complement to the garlands draping the stone balustrade. Callie's heart tripped as she mounted the marble stairs under the watchful eyes of what looked like ten or twelve generations of Carlo's ancestors.

Banks of poinsettias ringed the second-floor landing. As Carlo led her past the glorious color, Callie could hear an unseen baritone singing "Santa Lucia." She'd now adopted the hymn as her own personal anthem. The baritone was good, she acknowledged, but she intended to download Elvis's version the next time she logged into iTunes.

Then the same majordomo who'd met them downstairs opened a set of double doors. Beyond was a salon as long as the nave of a cathedral and almost as high ceilinged. Rows of gilt-edged chairs lined the salon's parquet floor. Callie blinked in surprise when she saw every seat was filled.

As though perfectly timed, the hymn finished and a string quartet launched into Mendelssohn's wedding march. Carlo squeezed Callie's arm and they followed Kate and Dawn down the aisle between the chairs. She smiled as she recognized the guests. Emilio and his crew. Marcello Audi, his daughter, Arianna, with her husband and kids. Sabeen and Leela and the other residents of the center. Amal and her baby in the second row with Simona.

Callie had to suppress a gasp at the director's altered appearance. Simona had tamed her flyaway hair and actually applied some lip gloss and blush. Even more astonishing, her floor-length skirt and fitted jacket of wine-colored velvet looked as though they might come from one of the boutiques on Via Condotti. Callie felt Carlo's start of surprise and had to hide a grin.

Travis and Brian and Tommy were in the front row. The men smiled and the boy beamed as Callie floated past. They were her family now, as much as Kate and Dawn. Integral threads in the fabric of her life.

But it was the man waiting for her at the end of the aisle who filled her heart. So tall, so awesome in his hand-tailored tux. Her very own Louis Jourdan, Callie thought with a lump in her throat.

"I must ask," the prince murmured, pressing her arm to his side. "Are you *sure* you're sure?"

She gave a helpless laugh. "Oh, Carlo. I've never been surer of anything in my life."

Then she put her hand in Joe's, and her Christmas wish came true.

* * * * *

Don't miss Dawn's and Kate's stories, part of the **THREE COINS IN THE FOUNTAIN** *miniseries:*

THIRD TIME'S THE BRIDE
"I DO"... TAKE TWO!

Available now wherever Special Edition books and ebooks are sold!

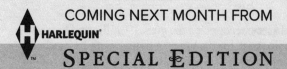

COMING NEXT MONTH FROM

HARLEQUIN®

SPECIAL EDITION

Available November 22, 2016

#2515 THE HOLIDAY GIFT
The Cowboys of Cold Creek • by RaeAnne Thayne
Neighboring rancher Chase Brannon has been a rock for Faith Dustin since her husband died, leaving her with two young children. Now Chase wants more. But Faith must risk losing the friendship she treasures and her hard-fought stability—and her heart—by opening herself to love.

#2516 A BRAVO FOR CHRISTMAS
The Bravos of Justice Creek • by Christine Rimmer
Ava Malloy is a widow and single mother who is not going to risk another heartbreak, but a holiday fling with hunky CEO Darius Bravo sounds just lovely! Darius wants to give her a Bravo under her tree—every Christmas. Can he convince Ava to take a chance on a real relationship or are they doomed to be a temporary tradition?

#2517 THE MORE MAVERICKS, THE MERRIER!
Montana Mavericks: The Baby Bonanza • by Brenda Harlen
Widowed rancher Jamie Stockton would be happy to skip Christmas this year, but Fallon O'Reilly is determined to make the holidays special for his adorable triplets—and for the sexy single dad, too!

#2518 A COWBOY'S WISH UPON A STAR
Texas Rescue • by Caro Carson
A Hollywood star is the last thing Travis Palmer expects to find on his ranch, so when Sophia Jackson shows up for "peace and quiet," he knows she must be hiding from something—or maybe just herself. There's definitely room on the ranch for Sophia, but Travis must convince her to make room in her heart for him.

#2519 THE COWBOY'S CHRISTMAS LULLABY
Men of the West • by Stella Bagwell
Widowed cowboy Denver Yates has long ago sworn off the idea of having a wife or children. He doesn't want to chance that sort of loss a second time. However, when he meets Marcella Grayson, he can't help but be attracted to the redheaded nurse and charmed by her two sons. When Marcella ends up pregnant, will Denver see a trap or a precious Christmas gift?

#2520 CHRISTMAS ON CRIMSON MOUNTAIN
Crimson, Colorado • by Michelle Major
When April Sanders becomes guardian of two young girls, she has no choice but to bring them up Crimson Mountain while she manages her friends' resort cabins. Waiting for her at the top is Connor Pierce, a famous author escaping his own tragedy and trying to finish his book. Neither planned on loving again, but will these two broken souls mend their hearts to claim the love they both secretly crave?

HSECNM1116

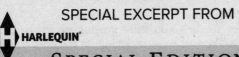
"You're the one who insisted this was a date-date. You
made a big deal that it wasn't just two friends carpooling
to the stock growers' party together, remember?"

"That doesn't mean I'm ready to start dating again, at
least not in general terms. It only means I'm ready to start
dating you."

There it was.

Out in the open.

The reality she had been trying so desperately to
avoid. He wanted more from her than friendship and she
was scared out of her ever-loving mind at the possibility.

The air in the vehicle suddenly seemed charged,
crackling with tension. She had to say something but had
no idea what.

"I… Chase—"

"Don't. Don't say it."

His voice was low, intense, with an edge to it she
rarely heard. She had so hoped they could return to the
easy friendship they had always known. Was that gone
forever, replaced by this jagged uneasiness?

"Say…what?"

"Whatever the hell you were gearing up for in that tone of voice like you were knocking on the door to tell me you just ran over my favorite dog."

"What do you want me to say?" she whispered.

"I sure as hell don't want you trying to set me up with another woman when you're the only one I want."

She stared at him, the heat in his voice rippling down her spine. She swallowed hard, not knowing what to say as awareness seemed to spread out to her fingertips, her shoulder blades, the muscles of her thighs.

He was so gorgeous and she couldn't help wondering what it would be like to taste that mouth that was only a few feet away.

She swallowed hard, not knowing what to say. He gazed down at her for a long, charged moment, then with a muffled curse, he leaned forward on the bench seat and lowered his mouth to hers.

Given the heat of his voice and the hunger she thought she glimpsed in his eyes, she might have expected the kiss to be intense, fierce.

She might have been able to resist that.

Instead, it was much, much worse.

It was soft and unbearably sweet, with a tenderness that completely overwhelmed her. His mouth tasted of caramel and apples and the wine he'd had at dinner—delectable and enticing—and she was astonished by the urge she had to throw her arms around him and never let go.

Don't miss
THE HOLIDAY GIFT by RaeAnne Thayne,
available December 2016 wherever
Harlequin® Special Edition books and ebooks are sold.

www.Harlequin.com

HSEEXP1116

THE WORLD IS BETTER WITH

Romance

Harlequin has everything from contemporary, passionate and heartwarming to suspenseful and inspirational stories.

Whatever your mood, we have romance when you need it, wherever you are!

HARLEQUIN®

A *Romance* FOR EVERY MOOD™

www.Harlequin.com

#RomanceWhenYouNeedIt

Reading Has Its Rewards
Earn **FREE BOOKS**!

Register at **Harlequin My Rewards** and submit your Harlequin purchases from wherever you shop to earn points for free books and other exclusive rewards.

Join for FREE today at **www.HarlequinMyRewards.com**.

JUST CAN'T GET ENOUGH?

Join our social communities
and talk to us online.

You will have access to the latest
news on upcoming titles and special
promotions, but most importantly,
you can talk to other fans about your
favorite Harlequin reads.

Harlequin.com/Community

Facebook.com/HarlequinBooks

Twitter.com/HarlequinBooks

Pinterest.com/HarlequinBooks

HSOCIAL